W9-AHR-982

THE CANDLES
OF YOUR EYES

Also by James Purdy

Novels

63: Dream Palace
Malcolm
The Nephew
Cabot Wright Begins
Eustace Chisholm and the Works
Jeremy's Version
I Am Elijah Thrush
The House of the Solitary Maggot
In a Shallow Grave
Narrow Rooms
Mourners Below
On Glory's Course
In the Hollow of His Hand

Poetry

An Oyster Is a Wealthy Beast
The Running Sun
Sunshine Is an Only Child
Lessons and Complaints

Stories and Plays

Color of Darkness
Children Is All
A Day After the Fair
Proud Flesh

THE CANDLES OF YOUR EYES

and thirteen other stories

JAMES PURDY

Weidenfeld & Nicolson
New York

Published by Weidenfeld & Nicolson, New York
A Division of Wheatland Corporation
10 East 53rd Street
New York, NY 10022

"Scrap of Paper" first appeared in *Evergreen Review,* "Mr. Evening" first appeared in *Harper's Bazaar, "On the Rebound"* was first published in the book of the same title by Black Sparrow Press, *"Some of These Days"* first appeared in *New Directions in Prose and Poetry 31,* "Summer Tidings" first appeared in *Esquire,* "Short Papa," "Sleep Tight," and "Mud Toe the Cannibal" first appeared in *The Antioch Review,* "How I Became a Shadow" first appeared in *New Directions Prose and Poetry No. 36,* "Ruthanna Elder" first appeared in *Barataria 4 Magazine,* "Lily's Party" first appeared in *Antaeus,* "Dawn" and "The Candles of Your Eyes" both first appeared in *Christopher Street Magazine,* and "Rapture" first appeared in *Second Coming* magazine.

Library of Congress Cataloging-in-Publication Data
Purdy, James. The candles of your eyes, and thirteen other stories.
I. Title.
PS3531.U426C33 1987 813'.54 86-19087
ISBN 1-55584-066-3

Manufactured in the United States of America
Designed by Paul Chevannes
First Edition
10 9 8 7 6 5 4 3 2 1

For Ron Holland

Contents

THE CANDLES
OF YOUR EYES

Some of These Days

What my landlord's friends said about me was in a way the gospel truth, that is he was good to me, and I was mean and ungrateful to him. All the two years I was in jail, nonetheless, I thought only of him, and I was filled with regret for the things I had done against him. I wanted him back. I didn't exactly wish to go back to live with him now, mind you, I had been too mean to him for that, but I wanted him for a friend again. After I got out of jail I would need friendship, for I didn't need to hold up even one hand to count my friends on, the only one I could even name was him. I didn't want anything to do with him physically again, I had kind of grown out of that somehow even more while in jail, and wished to try to make it with women again, but I did require my landlord's love and affection, for love was, as everybody was always saying, his special gift and talent.

He was at the time I lived with him a rather well-known singer, and he also composed songs, but even when I got into my bad trouble, he was beginning to go downhill, and not to be so in fashion. We often quarreled over his not succeeding way back then. Once I hit him when he told me how much he loved me, and knocked out one of his front teeth. But that was only after he had also criticized me for not keeping the apartment tidy and clean and doing the dishes, and I threatened him with an old gun I kept. Of course I felt awful bad about his losing this front tooth when he needed good teeth for singing. I asked his forgiveness. We made up and I let him kiss me and hold me tight just for this one time.

I remember his white face and sad eyes at my trial for breaking and entering and possession of a dangerous weapon, and at the last his tears when the judge sentenced me. My landlord could cry and not be ashamed of crying, and so you didn't mind him shedding tears somehow. At first, then, he wrote me, for as the only person who could list himself as nearest of kin or closest tie, he was allowed by the authorities to communicate with me, and I also received little gifts from him from time to time. And then all upon a sudden the presents stopped, and shortly after that, the letters too, and then there was no word of any kind, just nothing. I realized then that I had this strong feeling for him which I had never had for anybody before, for my people had been dead from the time almost I was a toddler, and so they are shadowy and dim, whilst he is bright and clear. That is, you see, I had to admit to myself in jail (and I choked on my admission), but I had hit bottom, and could say a lot of things now to myself, I guess I was in love with him. I had really only loved women, I had always told myself, and I did not love this man so much physically, in fact he sort of made me sick to my stomach to think of him that way, though he was a good-looker with his neat black straight hair, and his robin's-egg-blue eyes, and cheery smile. . . . And so there in my cell I had to confess what did I have for him if it was not love, and yet I had treated him meaner than anybody I had ever knowed in my life, and once come close to killing him. Thinking about him all the time now, for who else was there to think about, I found I got to talking to myself more and more like an old geezer of advanced years, and in place of calling on anybody else or any higher power, since he was the only one I had never met in my twenty years of life who said he cared. I would find myself saying like in church, *My landlord,* though that term for him was just a joke for the both of us, for all he had was this one-room flat with two beds, and my bed was the little one, no more than a cot, and I never made enough to pay him no rent for it, he just said he would trust me. So there in my cell, especially at night, I would say *My landlord,* and finally, for my chest begin to trouble me about this time and I was short of breath often, I would just manage to get out *My lord.* That's what I would call him for short. When I got out, the first thing I made up my mind to do was find him, and I was going to put all my efforts behind the search.

And when there was no mail now at all, I would think over all the kind and good things he done for me, and the thought would come to me which was blacker than any punishment they had given me here in the big house that I had not paid him back for his good deeds. When I got out I would make it up to him. He had took me in off the street, as people say, and had tried to make a man of me, or at least a somebody out of me, and I had paid him back all in bad coin, first by threatening to kill him, and then by going bad and getting sent to jail. . . . But when I got out, I said, I will find him if I have to walk from one ocean shore to the other.

And so it did come about that way, for once out, that is all I did or found it in my heart to do, find the one who had tried to set me straight, find the one who had done for me, and shared and all.

One night after I got out of jail, I had got dead drunk and stopped a guy on Twelfth Street, and spoke, *Have you seen my lord?* This man motioned to me to follow him into a dark little theater, which later I was to know all too well as one of the porno theaters, he paid for me, and brought me to a dim corner in the back, and then the same old thing started up again, he beginning to undo my clothes, and lower his head, and I jumped up and pushed him and ran out of the movie, but then stopped and looked back and waited there as it begin to give me an idea.

Now a terrible thing had happened to me in jail. I was beat on the head by another prisoner, and I lost some of the use of my right eye, so that I am always straining by pushing my neck around as if to try to see better, and when the convict hit me that day and I was unconscious for several weeks and they despaired of my life, later on when I come to myself at last, I could remember everything that had ever happened in my whole twenty years of life except my landlord's name, and I couldn't think of it if I was to be alive. That is why I have been in the kind of difficulty I have been in. It is the hardest thing in the world to hunt for somebody if you don't know his name.

I finally though got the idea to go back to the big building where he and I had lived together, but the building seemed to be under new management, with new super, new tenants, new everybody. Nobody anyhow remembered any singer, they said, nor any composer, and then after a time, it must have been though six months from the day I returned to New York, I realized that I had gone maybe to a building that just looked like the old building my landlord and I have lived in, and so I tore like a blue streak straightaway to this "correct" building to find out if any such person as him was living there, but as I walked around through the halls looking, I become somewhat confused all over again if this was the place either, for I had wanted so bad to find the old building where he and I had lived. I had maybe been overconfident of this one also being the correct place, and so as I walked the halls looking and peering about I become puzzled and unsure all over again, and after a few more turns, I give up and left.

That was a awesome fall, and then winter coming on and all, and no word from him, no trace, and then I remembered a thing from the day that man had beckoned me to come follow him into that theater, and I remembered something, I remembered that on account of my landlord being a gay or queer man, one of his few pleasures when he got an extra dollar was going to the porno movies in Third Avenue. My remembering this was like a light from heaven, if you can think of heaven throwing light on such a thing, for suddenly I knowed for sure that if I went to the porno movie I would find him.

The only drawback for me was these movies was somewhat expensive by now, for since I been in jail prices have surely marched upwards, and I have very little to keep me even in necessities. This was the beginning of me seriously begging, and sometimes I would be holding out my hand on the street for three-fourths of a day before I got me enough to pay my way into the porno theater. I would put down my three bucks, and enter the turnstile, and then inside wait until my eyes got used to the dark, which because of my prison illness took nearly all of ten minutes, and then I would go up to each aisle looking for my landlord. There was not a face I didn't examine carefully. . . . My interest in the spectators earned me several bawlings-out from the manager of the theater, who took me for somebody out to proposition the customers, but I paid him no mind. . . . But his fussing with me gave me an idea, too, for I am attractive to men, both young and old, me being not yet twenty-one, and so I began what was to become regular practice, letting the audience take any liberty they was in a mind to with me in the hopes that through this contact they would divulge the whereabouts of my landlord.

But here again my problem would surface, for I could not recall the very name of the person who was most dear to me, yes that was the real sore spot. But as the men in the movie theater took their liberties with me, which after a time I got sort of almost to enjoy, even though I could barely see their faces, only see enough to know they was not my landlord, I would then, I say, describe him in full to them, and I will give them this much credit, they kind of listened to me as they went about getting their kicks from me, they would bend an ear to my asking for this information, but in the end they never heard of him nor any other singer, and never knowed a man who wrote down notes for a living.

But strange as it might seem to anybody who will ever see these sheets of paper, this came to be my only connection with the world, my only life—sitting in the porno theater. Since my only purpose was to find him and from him find my own way back, this was the only thoroughfare there was open for me to reach him. And yet I did not like it, though at the same time even disliking it as much as I did, it give me some little feeling of a resemblance to warmth and kindness as the unknown men touched me with their invisible faces and extracted from me all I had to offer, such as it was. And then when they had finished me, I would ask them if they knew my landlord (or as I whispered to myself, my lord). But none ever did.

Winter had come in earnest, was raw in the air. The last of the leaves in the park had long blown out to sea, and yet it was not to be thought of giving up the search and going to a warmer place. I would go on here until I had found him or I would know the reason why, yes, I must find him, and not give up. (I tried to keep the phrase *My lord* only for myself, for once or twice when it had slipped out to a stranger, it give him a start, and so I watched what I said from there on out.)

And then I was getting down to the last of the little money I had come out of jail with, and oh the porno theaters was so dear, the admission was hiked another dollar just out of the blue, and the leads I got in that old dark hole was so few and far between.

Toward the end one man sort of perked up when I mentioned my landlord the singer, and said he thought he might have known such a fellow, but with no name to go on, he too soon give up, and said he guessed he didn't know after all.

And so I was stumped. Was I to go on patronizing the porno theater, I would have to give up food, for my panhandling did not bring in enough for both grub and movies, and yet there was something about bein' in that house, getting the warmth and attention from the stray men that meant more to me than food and drink. So I began to go without eating in earnest so as to keep up my regular attendance at the films. That was maybe, looking back on it now, a bad mistake, but what is one bad mistake in a lifetime of them.

As I did not eat now but only give my favors to the men in the porno, I grew pretty unsteady on my feet. After a while I could barely drag to the theater. Yet it was the only place I wanted to be, especially in view of its being now full winter. But my worst fears was now realized, for I could no longer afford even the cheap lodging place I had been staying at, and all I had in the world was what was on my back, and the little in my pockets, so I had come at last to this, and yet I did not think about my plight so much as about him, for as I got weaker and weaker he seemed to stand over me as large as the figures of the film actors that raced across the screen, and at which I almost never looked, come to think of it. No, I never watched what went on on the screen itself. I watched the audience, for it was the living that would be able to give me the word.

"Oh come to me, come back and set me right!" I would whisper, hoping someone out of the audience might rise and tell me they knew where he was.

Then at last, but of course slow gradual-like, I no longer left the theater. I was too weak to go out, anyhow had no lodging now to call mine, knew if I got as far as a step beyond the entrance door of the theater, I would never get back inside to its warmth, and me still dressed in my summer clothes.

Then after a long drowsy time, days, weeks, who knows? my worse than worst fears was realized, for one—shall I say day?— for where I was now there was no day or night, and the theater never closed its doors—one time, then, I say, they *come* for me, they had been studying my condition, they told me later, and they come to take me away. I begged them with all the strength I had left not to do so, that I could still walk, that I would be gone and bother nobody again.

When did you last sit down to a bite to eat? A man spoke this direct into my ear, a man by whose kind of voice I knew did not belong to the porno world, but come from some outside authority.

I have lost all tract of time, I replied, closing my eyes.

All right, buddy, the man kept saying, and *Now, bud,* and then as I fought and kicked, they held me and put the straitjacket on me, though didn't they see I was too weak and dispirited to hurt one cruddy man jack of them.

Then as they was taking me finally away, for the first time in months, I raised my voice, as if to the whole city, and called, and shouted, and explained: *"Tell him if he comes, how long I have waited and searched, that I have been hunting for him, and I cannot remember his name. I was hit in prison by another convict and the injury was small, but it destroyed my one needed memory, which is his name. That is all that is wrong with me. If you would cure me of this one little defect, I will never bother any of you again, never bother society again. I will go back to work and make a man of myself, but I have first to thank this former landlord for all he done for me."*

He is hovering between life and death.

I repeated aloud the word *hovering* after the man who had

pronounced this sentence somewhere in the vicinity of where I was lying in a bed that smelled strong of carbolic acid.

And as I said the word *hovering*, I knew his name. I raised up. Yes, my landlord's name had come back to me. . . . It had come back after all the wreck and ruin of these weeks and years.

But then one sorrow would follow upon another, as I believe my mother used to say, though that is so long ago I can't believe I had a mother, for when they saw that I was conscious and in my right mind, they come to me and begun asking questions, especially *What was my name.* I stared at them then with the greatest puzzlement and sadness, for though I had fished up his name from so far down, I could no more remember my own name now when they asked me for it than I could have got out of my straitjacket and run a race, and I was holding on to the just-found landlord's name with the greatest difficulty, for it, too, was beginning to slip from my tongue and go disappear where it had been lost before.

As I hesitated, they begun to persecute me with their kindness, telling me how they would help me in my plight, but first of all they must have my name, and since they needed a name so bad, and was so insistent, and I could see their kindness beginning to go, and the cruelty I had known in jail coming fresh to mind, I said, "I am Sidney Fuller," giving them you see my landlord's name.

"And your age, Sidney?"

"Twenty, come next June."

"And how did you earn your living?"

"I have been without work now for some months."

"What kind of work do you do?"

"Hard labor."

"When were you last employed?"

"In prison."

There was a silence, and the papers was moved about, then: "Do you have a church or faith?"

I waited quite a while, repeating his name, and remembering I could not remember my own, and then said, "I am of the same faith as my landlord."

There was an even longer silence then, like the questioner had been cut down by his own inquiry, anyhow they did not interrogate me any more after that, they went away, and left me by myself.

After a long time, certainly days, maybe weeks, they announced the doctor was coming.

He set down on a sort of ice-cream chair beside me, and took off his glasses and wiped them. I barely saw his face.

"Sidney," he began, after it sounded like he had started to say something else first, and then changed his mind. "Sidney, I have some very serious news to impart to you, and I want you to try to be brave. It is hard for me to say what I am going to say. I will tell you what we have discovered. I want you, though, first, to swallow this tablet, and we will wait together for a few minutes, and then I will tell you."

I had swallowed the tablet it seemed a long time ago, and then all of a sudden I looked down at myself, and I saw I was not in the straitjacket, my arms was free.

"Was I bad, Doctor?" I said, and he seemed to be glad I had broke the ice, I guess.

"I believe, Sidney, that you know in part what I am going to say to you," he started up again. He was a dark man, I saw now, with thick eyebrows, and strange, I thought, that for a doctor he seemed to have no wrinkles, his face was smooth as a sheet.

"We have done all we could to save you, you must believe us," he was going on as I struggled to hear his words through the growing drowsiness given me by the tablet. "You have a sickness, Sidney, for which unfortunately there is today no cure. . . ."

He said more, but I do not remember what, and was glad when he left, no, amend that, I was sad I guess when he left. Still, it didn't matter one way or another if anybody stayed or lit out.

But after a while, when I was a little less drowsy, a new man come in, with some white papers under his arm.

"You told us earlier when you were first admitted," he was saying, "that your immediate family is all dead. . . . Is there nobody to whom you wish to leave any word at all? . . . If there is such a person, we would appreciate your writing the name and address on each of these four sheets of paper, and add any instructions which you care to detail."

At that moment, I remembered my own name, as easily as if it had been written on the paper before me, and the sounds of it placed in my mouth and on my tongue, and since I could not give my landlord's name again and as the someone to whom I could bequeath my all, I give the inquirer with the paper my own real name:

James De Salles

"And his address?" the inquirer said.

I shook my head.

"Very well, then, Sidney," he said, rising from the same chair the doctor had sat in. He looked at me some time, then kind of sighed, and folded the sheaf of papers.

"Wait," I said to him then, "just a minute. . . . Could you get me writing paper, and fountain pen and ink to boot. . . ."

"Paper, yes. . . . We have only ball-point pens, though. . . ."

So then he brought the paper and the ball-point, and I have written this down, asking another patient here from time to time how to say this, or spell that, but not showing him what I am about, and it is queer indeed isn't it, that I can only bequeath these papers to myself, for God only knows who would read them later, and it has come to me very clear in my sleep that my landlord is dead also, so there is no point in my telling my attendants that I have lied to them, that I am really James De Salles, and that my lord is or was Sidney Fuller.

But after I done wrote it all down, I was quiet in my mind and heart, and so with some effort I wrote my own name on the only thing I have to leave, and which they took from me a few moments ago with great puzzlement, for neither the person was known to them, and the address of course could not be given, and they only received it from me, I suppose, to make me feel I was being tended to.

Scrap of Paper

I hadn't the slightest intention of pampering Naomi or conde-
scending to her in any way; the wages I paid her were far in advance
of their day when she came to me. I allowed her, for example, my
own reading material, and many a time I have invited her to a bite
of cake in my presence when she served me tea; all these things I
repeat now because the rumor she has been circulating that I
struck her for having faded my beautiful rose carpets from Portugal
is quite beside the point; what I did to Naomi could never, not even
in a court of law, be construed as striking. I merely slapped her. She
deserved it, she admitted she deserved it. She faded my carpets,
and she didn't care. But that was not the real crisis, and it did not
cause her to leave. Naomi had changed. She was not a double
personality, as some people call it, not a bit of it; Naomi had simply
become another woman from the pleasant, efficient, know-her-
place, very attractive though black as the ace of spades girl I took in
some twenty years ago.

"You're a woman of at least forty, though you lie to your men friends about your age!" I cried to her on that terrible April morning when she smashed the entire china closet before my eyes. "Why, oh why," I went on, nearly beside myself, "did you fade that beautiful pair of carpets from Portugal? . . . You willfully and deliberately exposed them to that pitiless sunlight. . . ." Then she threw the beautiful Dresden teapot straight at me. . . . I was calm. I said, "Naomi, if that had hit me, you would have gone to death row. . . ."

I paid her, of course, and never expected to set eyes on her again, but she returned. Wore a veil, and asked if she could bring her husband to visit. . . .

"What sort of a *young* man did you marry, may I ask?" I said, and she did not evidently like the long stress I had put on the word *young.*

"I married me a man, Mrs. Bankers," she replied.

"Naomi, my dear." I raised my hand as a warning, for my fingers were resting near my emergency telephone. "Remember," I said, "we are friends now."

Stung perhaps by the rudeness in her voice, I cried, "You are no more the Naomi who came to me in 1947 than you're a water buffalo!" I knew I had chosen a poor comparison. I had been reading something about the animal in a picture magazine, and it came unexpectedly to mind.

"Why do you compare me to a vicious Oriental beast of burden?" she inquired, and she stood up.

"Will you sit down, Naomi!" I cried. "And please lift up your veil. In *our* day," I could not help adding, "veils were worn only by Catholic ladies when in mourning. You're not Catholic and you are incapable of mourning for anybody. Besides, you never knew your family. . . . I asked you what sort of a young man you had married, and I wish you'd be civil enough to follow the rules of conversation, or bid me good morning."

Then I heard her words as clear as a gong: "A while back you throwed up to me in your nasty lady-way my age, and now you go into my dress, when these is the points you rest weakest on yourself, for you know as well as I that you are crowding eighty and that you never wore a stitch of clothes yet that couldn't be snapped up by the freak show."

"How dare you," I cried. "Speak so to a woman who provided you with your bread for twenty years!"

"And your advanced age, technically you are a ancient, and your odd getups are the least of it, for I won't mention nobody in and around this suite has ever thought you was anything but harmless-crazy! There!" she cried, and she got up and moved around the room to touch her glove on the windowsill and pretended to find dirt.

"Your house is filthy since I left you and you know it!" Naomi went on after a long wait on my part. "And don't you use the expression how-dare-you to me, 'cause I'm not in the mood for your old-fashioned smooth hellishness," she added.

"All right," I soothed her, for I felt gravely ill, and told her I felt so. "You'll fix me some tea," I informed her, "and you'll stay in case I have an attack. . . . Do you realize," I admonished her, "what you're doing to me? . . . You came here to kill me, in the cleverest way possible, and you know it."

"All you heiresses is tarred to the same stick: a honest day's work with your hands would have told you the difference between loafing-fatigue and heart ailment. . . ."

I sniffed at her words, said nothing more, and waited for her to prepare my tea. Naomi always prepared it so well, in fact she was a born cook, although of course I trained her. When she came to me she couldn't boil water, as they say. I trained her indeed in everything, and I paid for two of her abortions. I was a second mother to her.

"What do you pay this Norwegian charm woman works for you?" Naomi said, pouring me some tea.

"Are you going to kill me if I don't tell you, my dear?" I inquired of her.

"I already know anyhow, Miss Smarty," Naomi said.

"Now, you look here," I replied, getting really angry.

"I seen your Norwegian up the street the other day." Naomi ignored me. "Asked her right out after telling her who I was. She hesitated a minute and then she told me. I says, 'That's more than Mrs. Bankers paid me for a month backbreaking work.' "

"You ate a great deal while here, Naomi, don't forget," I reminded her.

"But here you are"—I could no longer contain myself—"at your old tricks of humiliating me in my own home!"

"Don't you work yourself up to that attack now, Mrs. Bankers, and then up and blame me; that's about the size of it; you'd like to work yourself to a stroke here and have the police think I brought it on."

"I want to be your friend, Naomi, and as I said earlier, I'm ready to meet your young husband."

"He ain't no youth, he's over thirty," she snapped at me. "You don't think I want me a youth, do you, after all the trouble I got in with the others, which, as you like to remind the world, you was so good at helping me out in."

"I'll meet him," I said.

"I never said one thing about bringing him." She was as tart as ever.

"Oh, Naomi, Naomi!" I cried.

Then I heard myself saying it, after all the insults the slut had poured on me. I heard myself saying, "Why don't you come back, Naomi?"

Do you know what she did, she laughed so hard you would have thought somebody knocked the wind out of her the way she finally had to gasp for breath.

"Oh, it's not that funny." I felt myself turning red.

"You don't care then I faded the rugs," Naomi started in again on that.

When I looked peaceable, she went on: "Let me tell you, Mrs. Bankers. I think them rugs was faded when you got them from your Great-aunt Betty, or whoever give them to you. It come from the camels faded."

"How would you know the condition of heirlooms!" I shot at her.

" 'Cause I know myself, and I know when people fib about themselves to me."

"You have no self!" I retorted. "You're a chameleon, and you're color-blind!"

"What did you say?" She became incoherent with rage, shouting at me.

"Oh forget it, why can't you?" I said to her. "I haven't an ounce of prejudice and you know it."

She laughed her terrible put-on nasty laugh.

"Naomi, Naomi," I now appealed to her. "Why can't you come to your senses and come back here to live? . . . That man you married surely can't love you. . . . I'll bet he's living off you. . . . Tell me if I'm not speaking the truth."

She gave me a very queer look, then poured me some more tea.

"Would you like me to fix you some toast, and open you a jar of some preserves. Noticed you had an unopened jar out there."

"Think somebody else with a well-known sweet tooth wants some preserves," I said. "Go ahead, do all the things you just said you'd do, including the opening of the preserves," I told her.

I waited till she brought everything in. "Naomi," I cried, "that is of course a wedding ring on your finger, let's see." She extended her hand and of course that was what it was, very nice gold in it too.

"I'm very put out you're married," I said.

She laughed pleasantly.

"Naomi, you should never have thrown that china pot at me that day," I told her.

"Now, now, Mrs. Bankers," she cautioned, and she sat down again in that damned costume and veil of hers.

"What nationality is this husband of yours, Naomi?" I ventured.

"Cuban."

"White?" I wondered.

"Oh, he's got several strains in him, Mrs. Bankers, including a dash of Chinese."

"You would," I sighed. "Well, it won't last, and you'll be back," I chided.

She fidgeted.

"Matter of fact, Mrs. Bankers," she began, and her face fell, "I'll let you in on a secret. It ain't lasted. It's over. . . . Now clap your little hands with joy."

"Then, my love, unless my name's not Mrs. Bankers, you're here as a suppliant!"

"As a what?"

"You heard me. You're here to beg your old job back when I no longer need you. When I've learned to get on without you!"

"Beggin'! Hear her! Huh-huh, Mrs. Bankers, Naomi don't have to beg, and you get that straight. I'm givin' you a offer."

Wreathed in pleasurable smiles, happy as I had not been in months, I confess, I drank another cup of tea.

"Tell you what," Naomi said, cautious, sweet. "I'll tell the tea leaves for you."

I hesitated, and she went on: "Bet that Norwegian bitch can't do that. She sure can't clean neither." She looked at the woodwork.

"You'll be mean to me if you come back!" I cried. "And oh, Naomi, God Almighty, can you be mean. You're the meanest woman ever drew breath when you are mean. . . . You've abused me sometimes until I thought I'd die. . . ."

"Mrs. Bankers, stop it."

"Some nights," I went right on, "I was in mortal fear you'd kill me."

"Monkey nuts!" she sneered. "I don't believe you was ever in mortal fear of anything anyhow!"

"Oh, Naomi, you'd persecute me if I let you back here, now you know you would. . . . Besides, maybe you killed your young Cuban husband, how do I know?"

"That little old punk isn't worth killin'," she mumbled.

"But," she went on, getting her ire up perhaps because she saw how I was smiling, "if you don't want me back, Mrs. Bankers, you don't and you know better than me that help like I can give is at a high bid today and scarcer than true love."

"Don't rub it in, Naomi." I felt myself bending. "Don't lord it over me. You will anyhow. But I ask you not to. You're cruel, and you're in control. What more can I say?"

"Honey, the day anybody is in control over you, they'll have the spots took out of leopards."

"Oh, don't be droll. You are anyhow. . . . God, I've missed your talk, Naomi. Sick to death of listening to foreigners. . . . Could your Cuban speak any known tongue outside of his own?"

"We didn't do much talking." Naomi smiled.

I stared at her, then merely said, "I expect not," and sighed.

I went on talking. "I've suffered so cruelly from insomnia since you went away," and I shaded my eyes. "All night long night after night awake listening to the boat whistles."

"Nobody to rub your poor little head." Naomi smiled.

"Nobody to do anything for me! While you lay in the arms of that Cuban . . . Naomi, a thing has occurred to me, knowing your temper. . . . You didn't kill him, did you? I won't keep an escaped murderess in my home! Did you come here because you've killed him?"

"I can see losin' me ain't changed you none, Mrs. Bankers. . . . Now hear my terms, dear heart. I'll come back if you'll sign a paper to the effect I never faded your rose rugs. . . ."

I looked at her to indicate I knew she had gone completely out of her mind.

"A little scrap of paper that I can keep," she went right on, "in case you turn ugly again and bring the subject up at a inopportune time."

"Naomi, child, who put you up to this?" I controlled myself.

"Did you ever know me to have to wait for somebody to put me up to anything, Mrs. Bankers. You must be losing your memory too!"

"Well, then what do you want me to sign a paper for!" I screamed at her.

She folded her arms, and oh the triumph on her mouth!

"Because," she went on, "I want *an* apology, that's why. And without *a* apology, I don't come back."

"Damn you, and damn your methods!" I cried, but I couldn't put any force in my voice, and oh did she observe that.

"What could I do with a old piece of paper that would simply say you, Celia Bankers, was mistaken in accusing Naomi Green of having faded your beautiful Portuguese rose rugs. With regret for having inconvenienced her, and then your signature."

Wiping my eyes, I said, "I'm surprised you wouldn't demand also that I put the date and place of my birth so that I could be further humiliated by a servant! . . . So then this is your reason! You came back here not to apologize yourself and ask for your job back, but to humiliate me in my own home, remind me again, as is your insane habit, of my age, and having insulted me, leave me again to the mercies of these sweating snooty standoffish irresponsible foreigners! Oh, Naomi, why did I ever take you in. Why did

I ever set eyes on you. I hate you. . . . Now, get out. You've had your sweet revenge."

"Now, now, sweetheart." She was as cool as a mountain spring, and took my cup out to the kitchen, got a fresh bigger one, filled it with strong hot tea, and put more bread in the toaster.

"Did your Cuban lover send you here to blackmail me?" I inquired, taking the tea.

"Don't try to change the subject, Mrs. Bankers."

"I won't write any absurd note abdicating from my natural rights and dignity so that you can show my statements to your lovers and laugh at me behind my back!"

"Miss Bankers! I'm warning you!"

"I'll never sign, you slut! Never."

"Miss Bankers, I'm going to have to punish you if you don't quit carryin' on like this."

"All the time I needed you and had to trust my person, my affairs, my very health and life to these no-account foreigners, you were lying in bed with a man and having to pay him for his favors to you! Don't interrupt me! That's how old you are now, and don't think I don't know it. You have to pay for it now at your age. You always have acted as if I knew nothing of the world. I know everything, you fool."

"Eat your toast and shut your mouth, Mrs. Bankers. I'm in no need of seeing you in one of your fits of hysterics, and I won't put up with it. You need me, you need me bad, you need me so bad I could make you take all your clothes off and crawl on hands and knees on your old faded carpets and say, 'Naomi! Come home!' "

"Yes, my carpets"—I looked down at them—"which of course I faded myself, or they came from the camels faded."

I began to cry hard then.

"I'm not taken in by your bawlin'," she scoffed.

"I didn't expect you to be." I blew my nose, and got really angry again. "A black whore like you."

Naomi laughed, and began waltzing around the room.

"Don't break anything now because you'll have to stay and work it out for nothing, remember."

"I'll stay as soon as you sign that paper."

Coming over to the little Italian marble-topped table on which her teacup and jam rested, Naomi put down a blank sheet of linen paper, with a quill pen, copiously dipped.

"Take that paper and pen away, you low conniving creature!" I cried, but I'm afraid I showed no force or decision.

"I'll raise your pay," I said suddenly.

"You bet you will, Mrs. Bankers."

"I'll never sign, though."

"I've never told a soul how old you are, and you know it," Naomi said.

"You don't know how old I am." I raised my voice now.

"And I never told nobody you was a bona fide virgin either, and had never been married. I never even told anybody your real name."

I laid my head back against the velvet of the chair and said, "Go ahead, blackmail me."

"I've been faithful to you, Mrs. Bankers, and you know it."

"I won't sign your paper. If I signed it, you'd make me sign more, sign my life away to you."

"I won't let you off the hook just the same. I have my pride about them rugs. You told everybody I faded them. It hurt my standing."

"With whom, pray tell!" I demanded.

"The doormen," she said, after thinking for quite a while.

"Those drunken Irish idiots! A lame excuse coming from you!"

There was a long, terrible silence, and then I said, "Go back to your Cuban lover. . . . I'll stay here and die with foreigners."

"If I go this time, Mrs. Bankers, I ain't never coming back."

I began crying again, and Naomi could see she had scared me good.

"You've humiliated me for twenty years." I had to take the handkerchief she offered me, my own was useless by now.

Naomi folded her arms and sat down.

"You have no respect for me, you've never acted like I was your employer, and you've blackmailed me over the years because you know my correct age and that I was never married. You also know my real name. . . . So what can I do? . . . You and your likes are taking over. I'm a prisoner in my own house and nation!"

"Rotgut! Mrs. Bankers, and you know it."

Then she took my hand, put the pen in it, and held my hand to the paper.

I pretended to scream.

"If you don't sign in two seconds, I'm going out that door and never darken it again, and you can go ahead with your threat to die with them Norwegians and Croats."

"But I don't even know what to write!" I appealed to her.

"Write this," she said: "*. . . I, Celia Bankers, confess I wrongfully accused my maid of twenty years' standing, Miss Naomi Green, of having faded my beautiful rose Portuguese carpets, causing her as a result to lose face with the people who run this building and to look bad in general, whereas my carpets were already faded before Naomi got here.*"

I had written all the words dutifully and then handed the sheet of paper to Naomi.

"God Almighty, you wrote it!" she said.

I looked at the wall. I was very pale.

Suddenly, hearing the tearing sounds, I looked up. Naomi had torn up what I had just written.

"My dear child," I cried, extending my right arm toward her.

Naomi kneeled down, and I caressed her hair in the folds of my skirt.

"I've been just wonderful to you from the start, Mrs. Bankers, and you got to admit it."

"Do you want me to sign a paper to that effect also?" I wondered. "For I may as well while the pen is still wet with ink. . . ."

"Now, now." Naomi stirred under my fingers.

"Oh, Naomi, how I hate foreigners. I never want one of them to touch me again as long as I live. . . . You're so beautiful, after all, child." I patted Naomi's cheek. "You're a black rose." I kissed her hair. "I'd sign anything, I guess, to have you back."

Naomi giggled.

"To think though you got married, and to a Cuban who's of course black," I said. "How inconsiderate you have always been. Naomi, you are a fool."

Naomi jerked her head up from my lap.

"Now what have I said?" I cried, on seeing the look of flashing anger in Naomi's eyes. "I declare you don't know how to behave for more than five minutes at a time. . . . Lie still, and don't get so excited, Naomi. . . . After all, my dear, if you were a big enough fool to come back here, I'm a bigger one to let you."

Summer Tidings

There was a children's party in progress on the sloping wide lawn facing the estate of Mr. Teyte and easily visible therefrom despite the high hedge. A dozen school-aged children, some barely out of the care and reach of their nursemaids, attended Mrs. Aveline's birthday party for her son Rupert. The banquet or party itself was held on the site of the croquet grounds, but the croquet set had only partially been taken down, and a few wickets were left standing, a mallet or two lay about, and a red and white wood ball rested in the nasturtium bed. Mr. Teyte's Jamaican gardener, bronzed as an idol, watched the children as he watered the millionaire's grass with a great shiny black hose. The peonies had just come into full bloom. Over the greensward where the banquet was in progress one smelled, in addition to the sharp odor of the nasturtiums and the marigolds, the soft perfume of June roses; the trees have their finest green at this season, and small gilt brown toads were about in the earth. The Jamaican servant hardly took his eyes off the children. Their gold heads and white summer clothing rose above the June verdure in remarkable contrast, and the brightness of so many colors made his eyes smart and caused him to pause frequently from his watering. Edna Gruber, Mrs. Aveline's secretary and companion, had promised the Jamaican a piece of the "second" birthday cake when the banquet should be over, and told him the kind thought came from Mrs. Aveline herself. He had nodded when Edna told him of his coming treat, yet it was not the anticipation of the cake which made him so absentminded and broody as it was the unaccustomed sight of so many young children all at once. Edna could see that the party had stirred something within his mind, for he spoke even less than usual to her today as she tossed one remark after another across the boundary of the privet hedge separating the two large properties.

More absentminded than ever, he went on hosing the peony bed until a slight flood filled the earth about the blooms and squashed onto his open sandals. He moved off then and began sprinkling with tempered nozzle the quince trees. Mr. Teyte, his employer and the owner of the property which stretched far and wide before the eye with the exception of Mrs. Aveline's, had gone to a golf tournament today. Only the white maids were inside his big house, and in his absence they were sleeping most of the day, or if they were about would be indifferently spying the Jamaican's progress across the lawn, as he labored to water the already refreshed black earth and the grass as perfectly green and motionless as in a painted backdrop. Yes, his eyes, his mind, were dreaming today despite the almost infernal noise of all those young throats, the guests of the birthday party. His long black lashes gave the impression of having been dampened incessantly either by the water from the hose or some long siege of tears.

Mr. Teyte, if not attentive or kind to him, was his benefactor, for somehow that word had come to be used by people who knew both the gardener and the employer from far back, and the word had come to be associated with Mr. Teyte by Galway himself, the Jamaican servant. But Mr. Teyte, if not unkind, was undemonstrative, and if not indifferent, paid low wages, and almost never spoke to him, issuing his commands, which were legion, through the kitchen and parlor maids. But once when the servant had caught pneumonia, Mr. Teyte had come unannounced to the hospital in the morning, ignoring the rules that no visits were to be allowed except in early evening, and though he had not spoken to Galway, he had stood by his bedside a few moments, gazing at the sick man as if he were inspecting one of his own ailing riding horses.

But Mrs. Aveline and Edna Gruber talked to Galway, were kind to him. Mrs. Aveline even "made" over him. She always spoke to him over the hedge every morning, and was not offended or surprised when he said almost nothing to her in exchange. She seemed to know something about him from his beginnings, at any rate she knew Jamaica, having visited there three or four times. And so the women—Edna and Mrs. Aveline—went on speaking to him over the years, inquiring of his health, and of his tasks with the yard, and so often bestowing on him delicacies from their liberal table, as one might give tidbits to a prized dog which wandered in also from the great estate.

The children's golden heads remained in his mind after they had all left the banquet table and gone into the interior of the house, and from thence their limousines had come and taken them to their own great houses. The blond heads of hair continued to swim before his eyes like the remembered sight of fields of wild buttercups outside the great estate, stray flowers of which occasionally cropped up in his own immaculate greensward, each golden corolla as bright as the strong rays of the noon sun. And then the memory came of the glimpsed birthday cake with the yellow center. His mouth watered with painful anticipation, and his eyes again filled with tears.

The sun was setting as he turned off the hose, and wiped his fingers from the water and some rust stains, and a kind of slime which came out from the nozzle. He went into a little brick shed, and removed his shirt, wringing wet, and put on a dry one of faded cotton decorated with a six-petaled flower design. Ah, but the excitement of all those happy golden heads sitting at a banquet —it made one too jumpy for cake, and their voices still echoed in his ears a little like the cries of the swallows from the poplar trees.

Obedient, then, to her invitation, Galway, the Jamaican gardener, waited outside the buttery for a signal to come inside, and partake of the birthday treat. In musing, however, about the party and all the young children, the sounds of their gaiety, their enormous vitality, lung power, their great appetites, the happy other sounds of silverware and fine china being moved about, added to which had been the song of the birds now getting ready to settle down to the dark of their nests, a kind of memory, a heavy nostalgia had come over him, recollection deep and far-off weighted him down without warning like fever and profound sickness. He remembered his dead loved ones. . . . How long he had stood on the back steps he could not say, until Edna, suddenly laughing as she opened the door on him, with flushed face, spoke: "Why, Galway, you know you should not have stood on ceremony. . . . Of all people, you are the last who is expected to hang back. . . . Your cake is waiting for you. . . ."

He entered and sat in his accustomed place where so many times past he was treated to dainties and rewards.

"You may wonder about the delay." Edna spoke more formally today to him than usual. "Galway, we have, I fear, bad news. . . . A telegram has arrived. . . . Mrs. Aveline is afraid to open it. . . ."

Having said this much, Edna left the room, allowing the swinging door which separated the kitchen from the rest of the house to close behind her and then continue its swing backwards and forwards like the pendulum of a clock.

Galway turned his eyes to the huge white cake with the yellow center which she had expressly cut for him. The solid silver fork in his hand was about to come down on the thick heavily frosted slice resting sumptuously on hand-painted china. Just then he heard a terrible cry rushing through the many rooms of the house and coming, so it seemed, to stop directly at him and then cease and disappear into the air and the nothingness about him. His mouth became dry, and he looked about like one who expects unknown and immediate danger. The fork fell from his brown calloused muscular hand. The cry was now repeated, if anything more loudly, then there was a cavernous silence, and after some moments, steady prolonged hopeless weeping. He knew it was Mrs. Aveline. The telegram must have brought bad news. He sat on looking at the untasted cake. The yellow of its center seemed to stare at him.

Edna now came through the swinging door, her eyes red, a pocket handkerchief held tightly in her right hand, her opal necklace slightly crooked. "It was Mrs. Aveline's mother, Galway. . . . She is dead. . . . And such a short time since Mrs. Aveline's husband died too, you know. . . ."

Galway uttered some words of regret, sympathy, which Edna did not hear, for she was still listening to any sound which might try to reach her from beyond the swinging door.

At last turning round, she spoke: "Why, you haven't so much as touched your cake. . . ." She looked at him almost accusingly.

"She has lost her own mother. . . ." Galway said this after some struggle with his backwardness.

But Edna was studying the cake. "We can wrap it all up, the rest of it, Galway, and you can have it to sample at home, when you will have more appetite." She spoke comfortingly to him. She was weeping so hard now she shook all over.

"These things come out of the blue." She managed to speak at last in a neutral tone as though she was reading from some typewritten sheet of instructions. "There is no warning very often, as in this case. The sky itself might as well have fallen on us. . . ."

Edna had worked for Mrs. Aveline for many years. She always wore little tea aprons. She seemed to do nothing but go from the kitchen to the front parlor or drawing room, and then return almost immediately to where she had been in the first place. She had supervised the children's party today, ceaselessly walking around, and looking down on each young head, but one wondered exactly what she was accomplishing by so much movement. Still, without her, Mrs. Aveline might not have been able to run the big house, so people said. And it was also Edna Gruber who had told Mrs. Aveline first of Galway's indispensable and sterling dependability. And it was Galway Edna always insisted on summoning when nobody else could be found to do some difficult and often unpleasant and dirty task.

"So, Galway, I will have the whole 'second' cake sent over to you just as soon as I find the right box to put it in. . . ."

He rose as Edna said this, not having eaten so much as a crumb. He said several words which hearing them come from his own mouth startled him as much as if each word spoken had appeared before him as letters in the air.

"I am sorry . . . and grieve for her grief. . . . A mother's death . . . It is the hardest loss."

Then he heard the screen door closing behind him. The birds were still, and purple clouds rested in the west, with the evening star sailing above the darkest bank of clouds as yellow as the heads of any of the birthday children. He crossed himself.

Afterwards he stood for some time in Mr. Teyte's great green backyard, and admired the way his gardener's hands had kept the

grass beautiful for the multimillionaire, and given it the endowment of both life and order. The wind stirred as the light failed,
and flowers which opened at evening gave out their faint delicate
first perfume, in which the four-o'clocks' fragrance was pronounced. On the ground near the umbrella tree something glistened. He stooped down. It was the sheep shears, which he
employed in trimming the ragged grass about trees and bushes,
great flower beds, and the hedge. Suddenly, stumbling in the
growing twilight, he cut his thumb terribly on the shears. He
walked dragging one leg now as if it was his foot which he had
slashed. The gush of blood somehow calmed him from his other
sad thoughts. Before going inside Mr. Teyte's great house, he put
the stained sheep shears away in the shed, and then walked quietly
to the kitchen and sat down at the lengthy pine table which was
his accustomed place here, got out some discarded linen napkins,
and began making himself a bandage. Then he remembered he
should have sterilized the wound. He looked about for some
iodine, but there was none in the medicine cabinet. He washed
the quivering flesh of the wound in thick yellow soap. Then he
bandaged it and sat in still communion with his thoughts.

Night had come. Outside the katydids and crickets had begun
an almost dizzying chorus of sound, and in the far distant darkness
tree frogs and some bird with a single often repeated note gave
the senses a kind of numbness.

Galway knew who would bring the cake—it would be the
birthday boy himself. And the gardener would be expected to eat
a piece of it while Rupert stood looking on. His mouth now went
dry as sand. The bearer of the cake and messenger of Mrs. Aveline's goodness was coming up the path now, the stones of gravel
rising and falling under his footsteps. Rupert liked to be near
Galway whenever possible, and like his mother wanted to give the
gardener gifts, sometimes coins, sometimes shirts, and now to-

night food. He liked to touch Galway as he would perhaps a horse. Rupert stared sometimes at the Jamaican servant's brown, thickly muscled arms with a look almost of acute disbelief.

Then came the step on the back porch, and the hesitant but loud knock.

Rupert Aveline, just today aged thirteen, stood with outstretched hands bearing the cake. The gardener accepted it immediately, his head slightly bowed, and immediately lifted it out of the cake box to expose it all entire except the one piece which Edna Gruber had cut in the house expressly for the Jamaican, and this piece rested in thick wax paper separated from the otherwise intact birthday cake. Galway fell heavily into his chair, his head still slightly bent over the offering. He felt with keen unease Rupert's own speechless wonder, the boy's eyes fixed on him rather than the cake, though in the considerable gloom of the kitchen the Jamaican servant had with his darkened complexion all but disappeared into the shadows, only his pale shirt and linen trousers betokening a visible presence.

Galway lit the lamp, and immediately heard the cry of surprise and alarmed concern coming from the messenger, echoing in modulation and terror that of Mrs. Aveline as she had read the telegram.

"Oh, yes, my hand," Galway said softly, and he looked down in unison with Rupert's horrified glimpse at his bandage—the blood having come through copiously to stain the linen covering almost completely crimson.

"Shouldn't it be shown to the doctor, Galway?" the boy inquired, and suddenly faint, he rested his hand on the servant's good arm for support. He had gone very white. Galway quickly rose and helped the boy to a chair. He hurried to the sink and fetched him a glass of cold water, but Rupert refused this, continuing to touch the gardener's arm.

"It is your grandmother's death, Rupert, which has made you upset. . . ."

Rupert looked away out the window through which he could see his own house in the shimmery distance; a few lamps had been lighted over there, and the white exterior of his home looked like a ship in the shadows, seeming to move languidly in the summer night.

In order to have something to do and because he knew Rupert wished him to eat part of the cake, Galway removed now all the remaining carefully wrapped thick cloth about the birthday cake and allowed it to emerge yellow and white, frosted and regal. They did everything so well in Mrs. Aveline's house.

"You are . . . a kind . . . good boy," Galway began with the strange musical accent which never failed to delight Rupert's ear. "And now you are on your way to being a man," he finished.

Rupert's face clouded over at this last statement, but the music of the gardener's voice finally made him smile and nod, then his eyes narrowed as they rested on the bloodstained bandage.

"Edna said you had not tasted one single bite, Galway." The boy managed to speak after a struggle to keep his own voice steady and firm.

The gardener, as always, remained impassive, looking at the almost untouched great cake, the frosting in the shape of flowers and leaves and images of little men and words concerning love, a birthday, and the year 1902.

Galway rose hurriedly and got two plates.

"You must share a piece of your own birthday cake, Rupert. . . . I must not eat alone."

The boy nodded energetically.

The Jamaican cut two pieces of cake, placed them on large, heavy dinner plates, all he could find at the moment, and produced thick solid silver forks. But then as he handed the piece of cake to Rupert, in the exertion of his extending his arm, drops of blood fell upon the pine table.

At that moment, without warning, the whole backyard was illuminated by unusual irregular flashing lights and red glares. Both Rupert and Galway rushed at the same moment to the window, and stared into the night. Their surprise was, if anything, augmented by what they now saw. A kind of torchlight parade was coming up the far greensward, in the midst of which procession was Mr. Teyte himself, a bullnecked short man of middle years. Surrounded by other men, his well-wishers, all gave out shouts of congratulation in drunken proclamation of the news that the owner of the estate had won the golf tournament. Suddenly his pals raised Mr. Teyte to their shoulders, and shouted in unison over the victory.

Listening to the cries growing in volume, in almost menacing nearness as they approached closer to the gardener and Rupert, who stood like persons besieged, the birthday boy cautiously put his hand in that of Galway.

Presently, however, they heard the procession moving off beyond their sequestered place, the torchlights dimmed and disappeared from outside the windows, as the celebrators marched toward the great front entrance of the mansion, a distance of almost a block away, and there, separated by thick masonry, they were lost to sound.

Almost at that same moment, as if at some signal from the disappearing procession itself, there was a deafening peal of thunder, followed by forks of cerise lightning flashes, and the air so still before rushed and rose in furious elemental wind. Then they heard the angry whipping of the rain against the countless panes of glass.

"Come, come, Rupert," Galway admonished, "your mother will be sick with worry." He pulled from a hook an enormous mackintosh, and threw it about the boy. "Quick, now, Rupert, your birthday is over. . . ."

They fled across the greensward where only a moment before the golf tournament victory procession with its torches had walked in dry, clear summer weather. Galway, who wore no covering, was immediately soaked to the skin.

Edna was waiting at the door, as constant in attendance as if she were a caryatid now come briefly to life to receive the charge of the birthday boy from the gardener, and in quick movement of her hand like that of a magician she stripped from Rupert and surrendered back to Galway his mackintosh, and then closed the door against him and the storm.

The Jamaican waited afterwards for a time under a great elm tree, whose leaves and branches almost completely protected him from the full fury of the sudden violent thundershower, now abating.

From the mackintosh, however, he fancied there came the perfume of the boy's head of blond hair, shampooed only a few hours earlier for his party. The odor came now swiftly in great waves to the gardener's dilating nostrils, an odor almost indistinguishable from the blossoms of honeysuckle. He held the mackintosh tightly in his hand for a moment, then drawing it closer to his mouth and pressing it hard against his nostrils, he kissed it once fervently as he imagined he saw once again the golden heads of the birthday party children assembled at the banquet table.

Mr. Evening

"You were asking the other day, Pearl, what that very tall young Mr. Evening—the one who goes past the house so often—does for a living, and I think I've found out for you," Mrs. Owens addressed her younger sister from her chair loaded with hand-sewn cushions.

Mrs. Owens continued to gaze out the big front window, its heavy shutter pulled back now in daylight to allow her a full view of the street.

She had paused long enough to allow Pearl's curiosity to whet itself while her own attention strayed to the faces of passersby. Indeed Mrs. Owens's only two occupations now were correcting the endless inventory of her heirlooms and observing those who passed her window, protected from the street by massive wrought-iron bars.

"Mr. Evening is in and out of his rooming house frequently enough to be up to a good deal, if you ask me, Grace," Pearl finally broke through her sister's silence.

Coming out of her reverie, Mrs. Owens smiled. "We've always known he was busy, of course." She took a piece of newsprint from her lap, and closed her eyes briefly in the descending rays of the January sun. "But now at last we know what he's busy at." She waved the clipping gently.

"Ah, don't start so, child." Mrs. Owens almost laughed. "Pray look at this, would you," and she handed the younger woman a somewhat lengthy "notice" clipped neatly from the *Wall Street Journal.*

While Pearl put on thick glasses to study the fine print, Mrs. Owens went on as much for herself as her sister: "Mr. Evening has always given me a special feeling." She touched her lavaliere. "He's far too young to be as idle as he looks, and on the other hand, as you've pointed out, he's clearly busier than those who make a profession of daily responsibility."

"It's means, Grace," Pearl said, blinking over her reading, but making no comment on it, which was a kind of desperate plea, it turned out, for information concerning a certain scarce china cup, circa 1910. "He has means," Pearl repeated.

"Means?" Mrs. Owens showed annoyance. "Well, I should hope he has, in his predicament." She hinted at even further knowledge concerning him, but with a note of displeasure creeping into her tone at Pearl's somewhat offhand, bored manner.

"I've telephoned him to appear, of course." Mrs. Owens had decided against any further "preparation" for her sister, and threw the whole completed plan at her now in one fling. "On Thursday, naturally."

Putting down the "notice" Pearl waited for Mrs. Owens to make some elaboration on so unusual a decision, but no elaboration came.

"But you've never sold anything, let alone shown to anybody!" Pearl cried, after some moments of deeply troubled cogitation.

"Who spoke of selling!" Mrs. Owens tightened an earring.

"And as to showing, as you say, I haven't thought that far.
. . . But don't you see, poor darling"—here Mrs. Owens's voice
boomed in what was perhaps less self-defense than self-explana-
tion—"I've not met anybody in half a century who wants heirlooms so bad as he." She tapped the clipping. "He's worded
everything here with one thought only in mind—my seeing it."

Pearl withdrew into incomprehension.

"Don't you see this has to be the case!" Here she touched the
"notice" with her fingers again. "Who else has the things he's
enumerated here? He's obviously investigated what I have, and
he could have inserted this in the want ads only in the hope it
would catch my eye."

"But you're certainly not going to invite someone to the house
who merely wants what you have!" Pearl found herself for the first
time in her life not only going against her sister in opinion, but
voicing something akin to disapproval.

"Why, you yourself said only the other night that what we
needed was company!" Mrs. Owens put these words adroitly now
in her sister's mouth, where they could never have been.

"But Mr. Evening!" Pearl protested against his coming, ignoring or forgetting the fact she had been quoted as having said
something she never in the first place had thought.

"Don't we need somebody to tell us about heirlooms! I mean
our heirlooms, of course. Haven't you said as much yourself time
after time?"

Mrs. Owens was trying to get her sister to go along with her,
to admit complicity, so to speak, in what she herself had brought
about, and now she found that Pearl put her mind and temper
against even consideration.

"Someone told me only recently"—Pearl now hinted at a side
to her own life perhaps unknown to Mrs. Owens—"that the
young man you speak of, Mr. Evening, can hardly carry on a
conversation."

Mrs. Owens paused. She had not been inactive in making her own investigations concerning their caller-to-be, and one of the things she had discovered, in addition to his being a Southerner, was that he did not or would not "talk" very much.

"We don't need a conversationalist—at least not about *them*," Mrs. Owens nearly snapped, by *them* meaning the heirlooms. "What we need is an appreciator, and the *muter* the better, say I."

"But if that's all you want him for!"—Pearl refused to be won —"why, he'll smell out your plan. He'll see you're only showing him what he can never hope to buy or have."

A look of deep disappointment tinged with spleen crossed Mrs. Owens's still-beautiful face.

"Let him *smell* out our plan, then, as you put it," Mrs. Owens chided in the wake of her sister's opposition, "we won't care! If he can't talk, don't you see, so much the better. We'll have a session of 'looking' from him, and his 'appreciation' will perk us up. We'll see him taking in everything, dear love, and it will review our own lifelong success. . . . Don't be so down on it now. . . . And mind you, we won't be here quite forever," she ended, and a certain hard majestical note in her voice was not lost on the younger woman. "The fact," Mrs. Owens summed it all up, "that we've nothing to give him needn't spoil for us the probability he's got something to give us."

Pearl said no more then, and Mrs. Owens spoke under her breath: "I haven't a particle of a doubt that I'm in the right about him, and if it should turn out I'm wrong, I'll shoulder all the blame."

~~~~~~

Whatever particle of a doubt there may have been in Mrs. Owens's own mind, there was considerably more of doubt and apprehension in Mr. Evening's as he weighed, in his rooming house, the rash decision he had made to visit formidable Mrs. Owens in—one could not say her business establishment, since she had none—but her background of accumulation of heirlooms, which vague world was, he could only admit, also his own. Because he had never known or understood people well, and he was the most insignificant of "collectors," he was at a loss as to why Mrs. Owens should feel he had anything to give her, and since her "legend" was too well known to him, he knew she, likewise, had nothing at all to give him, except, and this was why he was going, the "look-in" which his visit would give him. Whatever risk there was in going to see her, and there appeared to be some, he felt, from "warnings" of a queer kind from those who had dealt with her, it was worth something just to get inside, even though again he had been informed by those in the business it would be doubtful if he would be allowed to mention "purchase" and in the end it was also doubtful he would be allowed even a close peek.

On the other hand, if Mrs. Owens wanted him to tell her something—this crossed his mind as he went toward her huge pillared house, though he could not imagine even vaguely what he could have to tell her, and if she was mad enough to think him capable of entertaining her, for after all she was a lonely ancient lady on the threshold of death, he would disabuse her of all such expectations almost as soon as they had met. He was uneasy with old women, he supposed, though in his work he spent more time with them than with other people, and he wanted, he finally said out loud to himself, that hand-painted china cup, 1910, no matter what it might cost him. He fancied she might yield it to him at some atrocious illegal price. It was no more improbable, after all, than that she had invited him in the first place. Mrs. Owens never invited anybody, that is, from the outside, and the inside people in her life had all died or were incapacitated from paying calls. Yes, he had been summoned, and he could hope at least therefore that what everybody else told him was at least thinkable—purchase, and if that was not in store for him, then the other improbable thing, "viewing."

But Mr. Evening could not pretend. If his getting the piece of china or even more improbably other larger heirlooms, kept from daylight as well as human eyes, locked away in the floors above her living room, if possession meant long hours of currying favor, talking and laughing and dining and killing the evening, then no thank you, never. His inability to pretend, he supposed, had kept him from rising in the antique trade, for although he had a kind of business of his own here in Brooklyn, his own private income was what kept him afloat, and what he owned in heirlooms, though remarkable for a young dealer, did not make him a figure in the trade. His inconspicuous position in the business made his being summoned by Mrs. Owens all the more inexplicable and even astonishing. Mr. Evening was, however, too unversed both in people and the niceties of his own profession to be either sufficiently impressed or frightened.

Meanwhile Pearl, moments before Mr. Evening's arrival gazing out of the corner of her eye at her sister, saw with final and uncomfortable consternation the telltale look of anticipation on the older woman's face which demonstrated that she "wanted" Mr. Evening with almost the same inexplicable maniacal whim which she had once long ago demonstrated toward a certain impossible-to-find Spanish medieval chair, and how she had got hold of the latter still remained a mystery to the world of dealers.

~~~~~

"Shall we without further ado, then, strike a bargain?" Mrs. Owens intoned, looking past Mr. Evening, who had arrived on a bad snowy January night.

He had been reduced to more than his customary kind of silent social incommunicativeness by finally seeing Mrs. Owens in the flesh, a woman who while reputed to be so old, looked unaccountably beautiful, whose clothes were floral in their charm, wafting sachets of woody scent to his nostrils, and whose voice sounded like fine chimes.

"Of course I don't mean there's to be a sale! Even youthful you couldn't have come here thinking that." She dismissed at once any business with a pronounced flourish of white hands. "Nothing's for sale, and won't be even should we die." She faced him with a lessening of defiance, but he stirred uncomfortably.

"Whatever you may think, whatever you may have been told" —she went now to deal with the improbable fact of their meeting, —"let me say that I can't resist their being admired" (she meant the heirlooms, of course). She unfolded the piece of newsprint of his "notice." "I could tell immediately by your way of putting things"—she touched the paper—"that you knew all about them. Or better, I knew you knew all about them by the way you left things undescribed. I knew you could admire, without stint or reservation." She finished with a kind of low bow.

"I'm relieved"—he began to look about the large high room —"that you're not curious then to know who I am, to know about me, that is, as I'm afraid I wouldn't be able to satisfy your curiosity on that score. That is to say, there's almost nothing to tell about me, and you already know what my vocation is."

She allowed this speech to die in silence, as she did with an occasional intruding sound of traffic which unaccountably reached her parlor, but then at his helpless sinking look, she said in an attempt, perhaps, to comfort, "I don't have to be curious about anything that holds me, Mr. Evening. It always unfolds itself, in any case.

"For instance," she went on, her face taking on a mock-wrathful look, "people sometimes try to remind me that I was once a famous actress, which though being a fact, is irrelevant, and, more, now meaningless, for even in those remote days, when let's say I was on the stage, even then, Mr. Evening, these"—and she indicated with a flourish of those commanding white hands the munificent surroundings—"these were everything!"

"One is really only strictly curious about people one never intends to meet, I think, Mr. Evening," Mrs. Owens said.

She now rose and stood for a moment, so that the imposition of her height over him, seated in his low easy chair, was emphasized, then walking over to a tiny beautiful peachwood table, she looked at something on it. His own attention, still occupied with her presence, did not move for a moment to what she was bestowing a long, calm glance on. She made no motion to touch the object on the table before her. Though his vision clouded a bit, he looked directly at it now, and saw what it was, and saw there could be no mistake about it. It was the pale rose shell-like 1910 hand-painted china cup.

"You don't need to bring it to me!" he cried, and even she was startled by such an outburst. Mr. Evening had gone as white as chalk.

He searched in vain in his pockets for a handkerchief, and noting his distress, Mrs. Owens handed him one from the folds of her own dress.

"I won't ever beg of you," he said, wiping his brow with the handkerchief. "I would offer anything for the cup, of course, but I can't beg."

"What will you do then, Mr. Evening?" She came to within a few inches of him.

He sat before her, his head slightly tilted forward, his palms upturned like one who wishes to determine if rain is beginning.

"Don't answer"—she spoke in loud, gay tones—"for nobody expects you to do anything, beg, bargain, implore, steal. Whatever you are, or were, Mr. Evening—I catch from your accent you are Southern—you were never an actor, thank fortune. It's one of the reasons you're here, you are so much yourself."

"Now, mark me." Mrs. Owens strode past his chair to a heavy

gold-brocaded curtain, her voice almost menacing in its depth of resonance. "I've not allowed you to look at this cup in order to tempt you. I merely wanted you to know I'd read your 'notice,' which you wrote, in any case, only for me. Furthermore, as you know, I'm not bargaining with you in any received sense of the word. You and I are beyond bargaining with one another. Money will never be mentioned between us, papers, or signatures—all that goes without saying. But I do want something," and she turned from the curtain and directed her luminous gray eyes to his face. "You're not like anybody else, Mr. Evening, and it's this quality of yours which has, I won't say won me, you're beyond winning anybody, but which has brought an essential part of myself back to me by your being just what you are and wanting so deeply what you want!"

Holding her handkerchief entirely over his face now so that he spoke to her as from under a sheet, he mumbled, "I don't like company, Mrs. Owens." His interruption had the effect of freezing her to the curtain before her. "And company, I'm afraid, includes you and your sister. I can't come and talk, and I don't like supper parties. If I did, if I liked them, that is, I'd prefer you."

"What extraordinary candor!" Mrs. Owens was at a loss where to walk, at what to look. "And how gloriously rude!" She considered everything quickly. "Good, very good, Mr. Evening. . . . But *good* won't carry us far enough!" she cried, and her voice rose in a great swell of volume until she saw with satisfaction that he moved under her strength. The handkerchief fell away, and his face, very flushed, but with the eyes closed, bent in her direction.

"You don't have to talk"—Mrs. Owens dismissed this as if with loathing of that idea that he might—"and you don't have to listen. You can snore in your chair if you like. But if you come, say, once a week, that will more than do for a start. You could consider this house as a kind of waiting room, let's say, for a day that's sure and bound to come for all, and especially us. . . . You'd wait here, say, on Thursday, and we could offer you the room where you are now, and food, which you would be entitled to spurn, and all you would need do is let time pass. I could allow you to see, very gradually"—she looked hurriedly in the direction of the cup—"a few things here and there, not many at a visit, of course, it might easily unhinge you in your expectant state"—she laughed—"and certainly I could show you nothing for quite a while from up there," and she moved her head toward the floors above. "But in the end, if you kept it up, the visits, I mean, I can assure you your waiting would 'pay off,' as they say out there. . . . I can't be any more specific." She brought her explanation of the bargain to an abrupt close, and indicated with a sweeping gesture he might stand and depart.

~·~·~·~·~

Thursday, then, set aside by Mrs. Owens for Mr. Evening to begin attendance on the heirlooms, loomed up for the two of them as a kind of fateful, even direful, mark on the calendar; in fact, both the mistress of the heirlooms and her viewer were ill with anticipation. Mr. Evening's dislike of company and being entertained vied with his passion for "viewing." On the other hand, Mrs. Owens, watched over by a saddened and anguished Pearl, felt the hours and days speed precipitously to an encounter which she now could not understand her ever having arranged or wanted. Never had she lived through such a week, and her fingers, usually white and still as they rested on her satin cushions, were almost raw from a violent pulling on and off of her rings.

At last Thursday, 8:30 P.M., came, finding Mrs. Owens with one glass of wine—all she ever allowed herself, with barely a teaspoon of it tasted. Nine-thirty struck, ten, no Mr. Evening. Her lips, barely touched with an uncommon kind of rouge, moved in a bitter self-deprecatory smile. She rose and walked deliberately to a small ebony cabinet, and took out her smelling bottle, which she had not touched for months. Opening it, she found it had considerably weakened in strength, but she took it with her back to her chair, sniffing its dilute fumes from time to time.

Then about a quarter past eleven, when she had finished with hope, having struck the silk and mohair of her chair several castigating blows, the miracle, Mr. Evening, ushered in by Giles (who rare for him showed some animation), appeared in his heavy black country coat. Mrs. Owens, not so much frosty from his lateness as incredulous that she was seeing him, barely nodded. Having refused her supper, she had opened a large gilt book of Flaxman etchings, and was occupying herself with these, while Pearl, seated at a little table of her own in the furthest reaches of the room, was dining on some tender bits of fish soaked in a sauce into which she dipped a muffin.

Mr. Evening, ignored by both ladies, had sat down. He had not been drinking, Mrs. Owens's first impression, but his cheeks were beet-red from cold, and he looked, she saw with uneasy observation, more handsome and much younger than on his first call.

"I hate snow intensely." Mrs. Owens studied his pants cuffs heavy with flakes. "Yet going south somewhere"—it was not clear to whom she was speaking from this time on—"that would be now too much in the way of preparation merely to avoid winter wet. . . . At one time traveling itself was home to me, of course," she continued, and her hands fell on a massive yellowed ivory paper-opener with a larger than customary blade. "One was put up in those days, not hurled over landscape like an electric particle. One wore *clothes,* one 'appeared' at dinner, which was an occasion, one conversed, *listened,* or merely sat with eyes averted, one rose, was looked after, watched over, if you will, one was often more at home *going* in those days than when one remained home, or reached one's destination."

Mrs. Owens stopped, mortified by a yawn from Mr. Evening.

Reduced to a kind of quivering dumbness, Mrs. Owens could only restrain herself, remembering the "agreement."

A butler appeared wearing green goggles and at a nearly imperceptible nod from Mrs. Owens picked up a minuscule marble-topped gold inlaid table, and placed it within a comfortable arm's reach of Mr. Evening. Later, another servant brought something steaming under silver receptacles from the kitchen.

"Unlike the flock of crows in flight today"—Mrs. Owens's voice seemed to come across footlights—"I can remember *all* my traveling." She turned the pages of Flaxman with critical quickness. "And that means in my case the globe, all of it, when it was largely inaccessible, and certainly infrequently commented or written upon by tradespeople and typists." She concentrated a moment in silence as if remembering perhaps how old she was and how far off her travel had been. "I didn't miss a country, however unrecommended or unlisted by some guide or hotel bursar. There's no point in going now or leaving one's front door when every dot on the map has been ground to dust by somebody's heavy foot. When everybody is *en route*, stay home! . . . Pearl, my dear, you're not looking at your plate!"

Pearl, who had finished her fish, was touching with nearsighted uncertainty the linen tablecloth with a gleaming fork. "Wear your glasses, dear child, for heaven's sweet sake, or you'll stab yourself!"

Mr. Evening had closed his eyes. He appeared like one who must impress upon himself not to touch food in a strange house. But the china on his table was stunning, though obviously brand-new and therefore not "anything." At last, however, against his better judgment, he lifted one of the cups, then set it down noiselessly. Immediately the butler poured him coffee. Against his will, he drank a tablespoon or so, for after the wet and cold he needed at least a taste of something hot. It was an unbelievable brew, heady, clear, fresh. Mrs. Owens immediately noted the pleasure on his face, and a kind of shiver ran through her. Her table, ever nonpareil, might win him, she saw, where nothing in her other "offerings" tonight had reached him.

"After travel was lost to me," Mrs. Owens went on in the manner of someone who is dictating memoirs to a machine, "the church failed likewise to hold me. Even then" (one felt she referred to the early years of another century), "they had let in every kind of speaker. The church had begun to offer thought and problems instead of merging and repose. . . . So it went out of my life along with going abroad. . . . Then my eyes are not, well, not so bad as Pearl's, who is blind without glasses, but reading tires me more and more, though I see the natural world of objects better perhaps now than ever before. Besides, I've read more than most, for I've had nothing in life but time. I've read, in sum, everything, and if there's a real author, I've been through him often more than twice."

Mr. Evening now tried a slice of baked Alaska, and it won him. His beginning the meal backwards was hardly intentional, but he had looked so snowy the butler had poured the coffee first, and the coffee had suggested to the kitchen the dessert course instead of the entrée.

Noting that Mr. Evening did not touch his wine, Mrs. Owens thought a moment, then began again, "Drinking has never been a consolation to me either. Life might have been more endurable, perhaps, especially in this epoch," and she looked at her glass, down scarcely two ounces. "Therefore spirits hardly needed to join travel in the things I've eliminated. . . ." Gazing upwards, she brought out, "The human face, perhaps strangely enough, is really all that has been left to me," and after a moment's consultation with herself, she looked obliquely at Mr. Evening, who halted conveying his fork, full of meringue, to his mouth. "I need the human face, let's say." She talked into the thick pages of the Flaxman drawings. "I can't stare at my servants, though outsiders have praised their fetching appeal. (I can't look at what I've acquired, I've memorized it too well.) No, I'm talking about the unnegotiable human face. Somebody," she said, looking nowhere now in particular, "has that, of course, while, on the other hand, I have what he wants badly, and so shall we say we are, if not a match, confederates of a sort."

Time had passed, if not swiftly, steadily. Morning itself was advancing. Mr. Evening, during the entire visit, having opened his mouth chiefly to partake of food whose taste alone invited him, since he had already dined, took up his napkin, wiped his handsome red lips on it, though it was, he saw, an indignity to soil such a piece of linen, and rose. Both Mrs. Owens and her sister had long since dozed or pretended to doze by the carefully tended log fire. He said good night therefore to stone ears, and went out the door.

~~~~~~

It was the fifth Thursday of his visits to Mrs. Owens that the change which he had feared and suspected from the start, and which he was somehow incapable of averting, came about.

Mrs. Owens and her sister had ignored him more and more on the occasion of his "calls," and an onlooker, not in on the agreement, might have thought his presence was either distasteful to the ladies, or that he was too insignificant—an impecunious relative, perhaps—to merit the bestowal of a glance or word.

The spell of the pretense of indifference, of not recognizing one another, ended haphazardly one hour when Pearl, without any preface of warning, said in a loud voice that strong light was being allowed to reach and ruin the ingrain carpet on the third floor.

Before Mrs. Owens could take in the information or issue a command as to what might be done, if she intended indeed to do anything about protecting the carpet from light, she heard a certain flurry from the direction of the visitor, and turning saw what the mention of this special carpet had done to the face of Mr. Evening. He bore an expression of greed, passionate covetousness, one might even say a deranged, demented wish for immediate ownership. Indeed his countenance was so arresting in its eloquence that Mrs. Owens found herself, going against her own protocol, saying, "Are you quite all right, sir?" But before she had the words out of her mouth he had come over to her chair without waiting her permission.

"Did you say ingrain carpet?" he asked with great abruptness.

When Mrs. Owens, too astonished at his tone and movement, did not reply, she heard Mr. Evening's peremptory: "Show it to me at once!"

"If you have not taken leave of your senses, Mr. Evening," Mrs. Owens began, bringing forth from the folds of her red cashmere dress an enormous gold chain, which she pressed, "would you be so kind, I might even say, so decent, as to remember our agreement, if you cannot remember who I am, and in whose house you are visiting."

Then, quickly, in a voice of annihilating anger, loud enough to be heard on a passing steamship: "You've not waited long enough, spoilsport!"

Standing before her, jaws apart, an expression close to that of an idiot who has been slapped into brief attention, he could only stutter something inaudible.

Alarmed by her own outburst, Mrs. Owens hastened to add, "It's not ready to be shown, my dear, special friend."

Mrs. Owens took his hands now in hers, and kissed them gently.

Kneeling before her, not letting go her chill handclasp, looking up into her furrowed rouged cheeks, "Allow me one glimpse," he beseeched.

She extricated her hands from his and touched his forehead.

"Quite out of the question." She seemed almost to flirt now, and her voice had gone up an octave. "But the day will come" —she motioned for him to seat himself again—"before one perhaps is expecting it. You have only hope ahead of you, dear Mr. Evening."

Obeying her, he seated himself again, and his look of crestfallen abject submissiveness, coupled with fear, comforted and strengthened Mrs. Owens so that she was able to smile tentatively.

"No one who does not live here, you see, can see the carpet." She was almost apologetic for her tirade, certainly she was consoling.

He bent his head.

Then they heard the wind from the northeast, and felt the huge shutter on the front of the house struggle as if for life. The snow followed soon after, hard as hail.

Tenting him to the quick, Mrs. Owens studied Mr. Evening's incipient immobility, and after waiting to see whether it would pass, and as she suspected, noted that it did not, she rang for the night servant, gave the latter cursory instructions, and then sat studying her guest until the servant returned with a tiny decanter and a sliver of handsome glass, setting these by Mr. Evening, who lightly caressed both vessels.

"Alas, Mr. Evening, they're only new," Mrs. Owens said.

He did not remember more until someone put a lap robe over his knees, and he knew the night had advanced into the glimmerings of dawn, and that he therefore must have slept upright in the chair all those hours, fortified by nips from the brandy, which, unlike the glass that contained it, was ancient.

When morning had well advanced, he found he could not rise. A new attendant, with coal-black sideburns and ashen cheeks, assisted him to the bathroom, helped him bathe and then held him securely under the armpits while he urinated a stream largely blood. He stared into the bowl but regarded the crimson pool there without particular interest or alarm.

Then he was back in the chair again, the snow still pelted the shutters, and the east wind raved like lunatics helpless without sedation.

Although he was certain Mrs. Owens passed from time to time in the adjoining room—who could fail to recognize her tread, as dominating and certain as her resonant voice—she did not enter that day either to look at him or inquire. Occasionally he heard, to his acute distress, dishes being moved and, so it seemed, placed in straw.

Once or twice he thought he heard her clap her hands, an anachronism so imperial he found himself giggling convulsively. He also heard a parrot screech, and then almost immediately caught the sound of its cage being taken up and the cries of the bird retreating further and further into total silence.

Some time later he was served food so highly seasoned, so copiously sprinkled with herbs and spices that added to his disinclination to partake of food, he could not identify a morsel of what he tasted.

Then Giles reappeared, with a sterling-silver basin, a gleaming tray of verbena soap, and improbably enough, looking up at him, his own straight razor, for if it was one thing in the world of manhood he had mastered, it was to shave beautifully with a razor, an accomplishment he had learned from his captain in military school.

"How did they get my own things fetched here, Giles?" he inquired, with no real interest in having his question answered.

"We've had to bring everything, under the circumstances," Giles replied in a hollow vestryman's voice.

Mr. Evening lay back then, while he felt the servant's hands tuck a blanket about his slippers and thighs.

"Mrs. Owens thinks it's because your blood is thinner than we

Northerners that the snow affects you in this way." Giles offered
a tentative explanation of the young man's plight.

Suddenly from directly overhead, Mr. Evening heard carpenters, loud as if in the room with him, sawing and hammering. He
stirred uncomfortably in his stocking feet.

In the hall directly in line with his chair, though separated by
a kind of heavy partition, Mrs. Owens and two gentlemen of
vaguely familiar voices were doing a loud inventory of "effects."

Preparations for an auction must be in progress, Mr. Evening
decided. He now heard with incipient unease and at the same
time a kind of feeble ecstasy the names of every rare heirloom in
the trade, but these great objects' names were loudly hawked,
checked, callously enumerated, and the whole proceedings were
carried off with a kind of rage and contempt in the voice of the
auctioneer so that one had the impression the most priceless and
rarest treasures worthy finally of finding a home only in the
Louvre were being noted here prior to their being carted out in
boxes and tossed into the bonfire. At one point in the inventory
he let out a great cry of "Stop it!"

The partition in the wall opened, and Mrs. Owens stood staring at him from about ten feet away; then after a look of what
was meant perhaps to be total unrecognition or bilious displeasure, she closed the sliding panel fast, and the inventory was again
in progress, louder, if anything, than before, the tone of the
hawker's voice more rasping and vicious.

Following a long nap, he remembered two strangers, dressed
in overalls, enter with a gleaming gold tape; they stooped down,
grunting and querulous, and made meticulous if furtive movements of measuring him from head to toe, his sitting posture
requiring them, evidently, to check their results more than once.

Was it now Friday night, or had the weekend already passed,
and were we arrived at Monday?

The snow had continued unabated, so far as his memory

served, though the wind was weaker, or more fitful, and the shutters nearly silent. He supposed all kinds of people had called on him at his lodgings. Then Giles appeared again, after Mr. Evening had passed more indistinct hours in his chair, and the servant helped him into the toilet, where he passed thick clots of blood, and on his return to his chair, Mr. Evening found himself face to face with his own large steamer trunk and a pair of valises.

While he kept his eyes averted from the phenomenal appearance of his luggage, Giles combed and cut his long chestnut hair, trimmed the shagginess of his eyebrows, and massaged the back of his neck. Mr. Evening did not ask him if there was any reason or occasion for tonsorial attention, but at last he did inquire, more for breaking the lugubrious silence than for getting any pertinent answer, "What was the carpentering upstairs for, Giles?"

The servant hesitated, stammered, and in his confusion came near nipping Mr. Evening's ear with the barber's shears, but at last answered the question in a loud whisper: "They're remodeling the bed."

The room in which he had sat these past days, however many, four, six, a fortnight, perhaps, the room which had been Mrs. Owens's and her sister's on those first Thursday nights of his visits, was now only his alone, and the two women had passed on to other quarters in a house whose chambers were, like its heirlooms, difficult, perhaps impossible, to number.

Limited to a kind of speechless listlessness—he assumed he must be very ill, though he did not wonder why no doctor came —and passing several hours without attendance, suddenly, in pique at being neglected, he employed Mrs. Owens's own queer custom and clapped his hands peremptorily. A dark-skinned youth with severe bruises about his temples appeared and, without inquiry or greeting, adjusted Mr. Evening's feet on a stool, poured him a drink of something red with a bitter taste, and, while he waited for the sick man to drink, made a gesture of inquiry as to whether Mr. Evening wished to relieve himself.

More indistinct hours swam slowly into blurred unremembrance. At last the hammering, pounding, moving of furniture, together with the suffocating fumes of turpentine and paint, all ceased to molest him.

Mrs. Owens, improbably, appeared again, accompanied by Pearl.

"I am glad to see you better, Mr. Evening, needless to say," Mrs. Owens began icily, and one could see at once that she appeared some years younger, perhaps strong sunlight—now pouring in—flattered her, or could it be, he wondered, she had had recourse to plastic surgery during his illness, at any rate, she was much younger, while her voice was harsher, harder, more actresslike than ever before.

"Because of your splendid recovery, we are therefore ready to move you into your room," Mrs. Owens went on, "where, I'm glad to report, you'll find more than one ingrain carpet spread out for you to rest your eyes on. . . . The bed," she added after a careful pause, "I do hope will meet with your approval" (here he attempted to say something contradictory, but she indicated she would not allow it), "for its refashioning has cost all of us here some pains to make over." Here he felt she would have used the word *heirloom*, but prevented herself from doing so. She said only, in conclusion, "You're over, do you realize, six foot six in your stocking feet!"

She studied him closely. "We couldn't let you lie with your legs hanging out of the bedclothes!

"Now, sir"—Mrs. Owens folded her arms—"can you move, do you suppose, to the next floor, provided someone, of course, assists you?"

The next thing he remembered was being helped up the interminable winding staircase by a brace of servants, while Mrs. Owens and Pearl brought up the rear, Mrs. Owens talking away:

"Those of us who are Northerners, Mr. Evening, have of course the blood from birth to take these terribly snowy days, Boreas and his blasts, the sight of Orion climbing the winter night, but our friends of Southern birth must be more careful. That is why we take such good care of you. You should have come, in any case, from the beginning and not kept picking away at a mere Thursday call," she ended on a scolding note.

The servants deposited Mr. Evening on a large horsehair sofa which in turn faced the longest bed he had ever set eyes on, counting any, he was certain, he had ever stared at in museums. And now it must be confessed that Mr. Evening, for all the length of him, had never from early youth slept in the kind of bed that his height and build required, for after coming into his fortune, he had continued to live in lodging houses which did not provide anything adequate for his physical measurements. Here at Mrs. Owens's, where his living was all unchosen by him, he now saw the bed perfectly suited for his frame.

A tiny screen was thrown up around the horsehair sofa, and while Mrs. Owens and Pearl waited as if for a performance to begin, Cole, a Norwegian, as it turned out, quietly got Mr. Evening's old business clothes off, and clad him in gleaming green and shell silk pajamas, and in a lightning single stride across the room carried the invalid to the bed, propped him up in a layer of cushions and pillows so that he looked as a matter of fact more seated now than when he had spent those days and nights in the big chair downstairs.

Although food had been brought for all of them, seated in different sections of the immense room, that is for Pearl, Mrs. Owens, and Mr. Evening, only Pearl partook of any. Mr. Evening, sunk in cushions, looked nowhere in particular, certainly not at his food. Mrs. Owens, ignoring her own repast (some sort of roast game), produced from the folds of her organdy gown a jewel-studded lorgnette, and began reading aloud in droning monotone a list of rare antiques, finally naming with emphasis a certain ormolu clock, which caused Mr. Evening to cry out, "If you please, read no more while I am dining!," although he had not touched a morsel.

Mrs. Owens put down the paper, waved it against her like a fan, and having put away her lorgnette came over to the counterpane of the bed.

She bent over him like a physician and he closed his eyes. The scent which came from her bosom was altogether like that of a garden by the sea.

"Our whole life together, certainly," she began, like one talking in her sleep, "was to have been an enumeration of effects. I construed it so at any rate. . . . I had thought," she went on, "that you would be attentive. . . . I procured these special glasses"— she touched the lorgnette briefly—"and if I may be allowed an explanation, I thought I would read to you since I no longer read to myself, and may I confess it, while I lifted my eyes occasionally from the paper, I hoped to rest them by letting them light on your fine features. . . . If you are to deprive me of that pleasure, dear Mr. Evening, say so, and new arrangements and new preparations can be made."

She pressed her hand now on the bed, as if to test its quality.

"I do not think even so poor an observer and so indifferent a guest as yourself can be unaware of the stupendous animation, movement, preparation, the entire metamorphosis indeed which your coming here has entailed. Mark me, I am willing to do more for you, but if I am to be deprived of the simple and may I say sole pleasure left to me, reading a list of precious heirlooms and at the same time resting my eyes from time to time on you, then say so, then excuse me, pray, and allow me to depart from my own house."

Never one endowed with power over language, Mr. Evening, at this, the most dramatic moment in his life, could only seize

Mrs. Owens's pliant bejeweled hand in his rough, chapped one, hold her finger to his face, and cry, "No!"

"No what?" she said, withdrawing her hand, a tiny indication of pleasure, however, moving her lips.

Raising himself up from the hillock of cushions, he got out, "What about the things I was doing out there," and he pointed haphazardly in the direction of where he thought his shop might possibly lie.

Mrs. Owens shook her head. "Whatever you did out there, Mr. Evening"—she looked down at him—"or, rather, amend that, sir, to this; you are now doing whatever and more than you could have ever done elsewhere. . . . This is your home!" she cried, and as if beside herself, "Your work is here, and only here!"

"Am I as ill as everything points to?" He turned to Pearl, who continued to dine.

Pearl looked to her sister for instructions.

"I don't know how you could be so self-centered as to talk about a minor upset of the urinary tract as illness"—Mrs. Owens raised her voice—"especially when we have prepared a list like this"—she tapped with her lorgnette on the inventory of antiques —"which you can't be ass enough not to know will one day be yours!"

Mrs. Owens stood up and fixed him with her gaze.

Mr. Evening's eyes fell then like dropping balls to the floor, where the unobtainable ingrain carpets, unobserved by him till then, rested beneath them like live breathing things. He wept shamelessly and Mrs. Owens restrained what might have been a grin.

He dried his eyes slowly on the napkin which she had proffered him.

"If you would have at least the decency to pretend to drink your coffee, you would see your cup," she said.

"Yes," she sighed, as she studied Mr. Evening's disoriented

features as he now caught sight of the 1910 hand-painted cup within his very fingertip, unobserved by him earlier, as had been the ingrain carpets. "Yes," Mrs. Owens continued, "while I have gained back my eyesight, as it were"—she raised her lorgnette briefly—"others are to all practical purposes sand-blind . . . Pearl" —she turned to her sister—"you may be excused from the room."

"My dear Mr. Evening," Mrs. Owens said, her voice materially altered once Pearl had disappeared.

He had put down the 1910 cup, perhaps because it seemed unthinkable to drink out of anything so irreplaceable, and so delicate that a mere touch of his lips might snap it.

"You can't possibly now go out of my life." Mrs. Owens half-stretched out her hand to him.

He supposed she had false teeth, they were too splendid for real, yet all of her suddenly was splendid, and from her person again came a succession of wild fragrance, honeysuckle, jasmine, flowers without names, one perfume succeeding another in enervating succession, as various as all her priceless heirlooms.

"Winter, even to a Southerner, dear Mr. Evening, can offer some tender recompense, and for me, whose blood, if I may be allowed to mention it again, is incapable of thinning." Here she turned down the bedclothes clear to his feet. The length of his feet and the beautiful architecture of his bare instep caused her for a moment to hesitate.

"I'm certain," she kept her words steady, placing an icy hand under the top of his pajamas, and letting it rest, as if in permanent location on his breast, "that you are handsome to the eye all over."

His teeth chattered briefly, as he felt her head come down on him so precipitously, but she seemed content merely to rest on his bare chest. He supposed he would catch an awful cold from it all, but he did not move, hearing her say, "And after I'm gone, all—all of it will be yours, and all I ask in return, Mr. Evening, is that all days be Thursday from now on."

He lay there without understanding how it had occurred, whether a servant had entered or her hands with the quickness of hummingbirds had done the trick, but there he was naked as he had come into the world, stretched out in the bed that was his exact length at last and which allowed him to see just what an unusually tall young man he was indeed.

Lily's Party

As Hobart came through the door of Crawford's Home Dinette, his eyes fell direct on Lily sitting alone at one of the big back tables, eating a piece of pie.

"Lily! Don't tell me! You're supposed to be in Chicago!" he ejaculated.

"Who supposed I was to be?" Lily retorted, letting her fork cut quickly into the pie.

"Well, I'll damn me if—" He began to speak in a humming sort of way while pulling out a chair from under her table, and sitting down unbidden. "Why, everybody thought you went up there to be with Edward."

"Edward! He's the last person on this earth I would go any-where to be with. And I think you know that!" Lily never showed anger openly, and if she was angry now, at least she didn't let it stop her from enjoying her pie.

"Well, Lily, we just naturally figured you had gone to Chicago when you weren't around."

"I gave your brother Edward two of the best years of my life."
Lily spoke with the dry accent of someone testifying in court for
a second time. "And I'm not about to go find him for more of
what he gave me. Maybe you don't remember what I got from
him, but I do. . . ."

"But where were you, Lily? . . . We all missed you!" Hobart
harped on her absence.

"I was right here all the time, Hobart, for your information."
As she said this, she studied his mouth somewhat absentmindedly. "But as to your brother, Edward Starr," she continued, and
then paused as she kept studying his mouth as if she found a
particular defect there which had somehow escaped scrutiny hith-
erto. "As to Edward," she began again, and then stopped, struck
her fork gingerly against the plate, "he was a number-one poor
excuse for a husband, let me tell you. He left me for another
woman, if you care to recall, and it was because of his neglect that
my little boy passed away. . . . So let's say I don't look back on
Edward, and am not going to any Chicago to freshen up on my
recollections of him. . . ."

She quit studying his mouth, and looked out the large front
window through which the full October moon was beginning its
evening climb.

"At first I will admit I was lonesome, and with my little boy
lying out there in the cemetery, I even missed as poor an excuse
for a man as Edward Starr, but believe you me, that soon passed."

She put down her fork now that she had eaten all the pie, laid
down some change on the bare white ash wood of the table, and
then, closing her purse, sighed, and softly rose.

"I only know," Lily began, working the clasp on her purse,
"that I have begun to find peace now. . . . Reverend McGilead,
as you may be aware, has helped me toward the light. . . ."

"I have heard of Reverend McGilead," Hobart said in a voice

so sharp she looked up at him while he held the screen door open for her.

"I am sure you have heard nothing but good then," she shot back in a voice that was now if not deeply angry, certainly unsteady.

"I will accompany you home, Lily."

"You'll do no such thing, Hobart. . . . Thank you, and good evening."

He noticed that she was wearing no lipstick, and that she did not have on her wedding ring. She also looked younger than when she had been Edward Starr's wife.

"You say you have found peace with this new preacher." Hobart spoke after her retreating figure. "But under this peace, you hate Edward Starr," he persisted. "All you said to me tonight was fraught with hate."

She turned briefly and looked at him, this time in the eyes. "I will find my way, you can rest assured, despite your brother and you."

He stayed in front of the door of the dinette and watched her walk down the moonlit-white road toward her house that lay in deep woods. His heart beat violently. All about where he stood were fields and crops and high trees, and the sailing queen of heaven was the only real illumination after one went beyond the dinette. No one came down this small road with the exception of lovers who occasionally used it for their lane.

Well, Lily is a sort of mystery woman, he had to admit to himself. And where, then, did the rumor arise that she had been to Chicago. And now he felt she had lied to him, that she had been in Chicago after all and had just got back.

Then without planning to do so, hardly knowing indeed he was doing so, he began following after her from a conveniently long distance down the moonlit road. After a few minutes of pursuing

her, he saw someone come out from one of the ploughed fields.
The newcomer was a tall still-youthful man with the carriage of
an athlete rather than that of a farmer. He almost ran toward Lily.
Then they both stopped for a moment, and after he had touched
her gently on the shoulder they went on together. Hobart's heart
beat furiously, his temple throbbed, a kind of film formed over his
lips from his mouth rushing with fresh saliva. Instead of following
them directly down the road, he now edged into the fields and
pursued them more obliquely. Sometimes the two ahead of him
would pause, and there was some indication the stranger was
about to leave Lily, but then from something they said to one
another, the couple continued on together. Hobart would have
liked to get closer to them so that he might hear what they were
saying, but he feared discovery. At any rate, he could be sure of
one thing, the man walking with her was not Edward, and also
he was sure that whoever he was he was her lover. Only lovers
walked that way together, too far apart at one time, too weaving
and close together another time: their very breathing appeared
uneven and heavy the way their bodies swayed. Yes, Hobart
realized, he was about to see love being made, and it made him
walk unsteadily, almost to stumble. He only hoped he could keep
a rein on his feelings and would not make his presence known to
them.

When he saw them at last turn into her cottage he longed for
the strength to leave them, to go back home to forget Lily, forget
his brother Edward, whom he was certain Lily had been "cheat-
ing" all through their marriage (even *he* had been intimate once
with Lily when Edward was away on a trip, so that he had always
wondered if the child she bore him in this marriage might not
have been after all his, but since it was dead, he would not think
of it again).

Her cottage had a certain fame. There were no other houses
about, and the windows of her living room faced the thick forest.

Here she could have done nearly whatever she liked and nobody would have been the wiser, for unless one had stood directly before the great window which covered almost the entire width of her room, any glimpse within was shut out by foliage, and sometimes by heavy mist.

Hobart knew that this man, whoever he was, had not come tonight for the purpose of imparting Jesus' love to her but his own. He had heard things about the young preacher, Reverend McGilead, he had been briefed on his "special" prayer meetings, and had got the implication the man of the cloth had an excess of unburned energy in his makeup. He shouted too loud during his sermons, people said, and the veins in his neck were ready to burst with the excess of blood that ran through him.

From Hobart's point of observation, in the protection of a large spruce tree, nothing to his surprise he saw whom he believed to be the young preacher take her in his arms. But then what happened was unforeseen, undreamed of indeed, for with the rapidity of a professional gymnast, the preacher stripped off his clothing in a trice, and stood in the clear illumination of her room not covered by so much as a stitch or thread. Lily herself looked paralyzed, as rodents are at the sudden appearance of a serpent. Her eyes were unfocused on anything about her, and she made no attempt to assist him as he partially undressed her. But from the casual way he acted, it was clear they had done this before. Yes, Hobart confessed to himself, in the protective dark of the tree under which he stood, one would have expected certainly something more gradual from lovers. He would have thought that the young preacher would have talked to her for at least a quarter of an hour, that he would have finally taken her hand, then perhaps kissed her, and then oh so slowly and excitingly, for Hobart at least, would have undressed her, and taken her to himself.

But this gymnast's performance quite nonplussed the observer by the spruce tree. For one thing, the gross size of the preacher's sex, its bulging veins and unusual angry redness, reminded him of sights seen by him when he had worked on a farm. It also recalled a surgical operation he had witnessed performed by necessity in a doctor's small, overcrowded office. The preacher now had pushed Lily against the wall, and worked vigorously at, and then through, her. His eyes rolled like those of a man being drawn unwillingly into some kind of suction machine, and saliva suddenly poured out of his mouth in great copiousness so that he resembled someone blowing up an enormous balloon. His neck and throat were twisted convulsively, and his nipples tightened as if they were being given over to rank torture.

At this moment, Hobart, without realizing he was doing so, came out from his hiding place, and strode up to the window, where he began waving his arms back and forth in the manner of a man flagging a truck. (Indeed Lily later was to believe that she thought she had seen a man with two white flags in his hands signaling for help.)

Lily's screams at being discovered broke the peace of the neighborhood, and many watchdogs from about the immediate vicinity began barking in roused alarm.

"We are watched!" she was finally able to get out. Then she gave out three uncadenced weak cries. But the preacher, his back to the window, like a man in the throes of some grave physical malady, could only concentrate on what his body dictated to him, and though Lily now struggled to be free of him, this only secured him the more tightly to her. Her cries now rose in volume until they reached the same pitch as that of the watchdogs.

Even Hobart, who had become as disoriented perhaps as the couple exhibited before him, began making soft outcries, and he continued to wave his arms fruitlessly.

"No, no, and no!" Lily managed now to form and speak these words. "Whoever you are out there, go, go away at once!"

Hobart now came directly up to the window. He had quit waving his arms, and he pressed his nose and mouth against the pane.

"It's me," he cried reassuringly. "Hobart, Edward Starr's brother! Can't you see?" He was, he managed to realize, confused as to what he now should do or say, but he thought that since he had frightened them so badly and so seriously disturbed their pleasure, he had best identify himself, and let them know he meant no harm. But his calling to them only terrified Lily the more, and caused her young partner to behave like someone struggling in deep water.

"Hobart Starr here!" the onlooker called to them, thinking they may have mistook him for a housebreaker.

"Oh merciful Lord," Lily moaned. "If it is you, Hobart Starr, please go away. Have that much decency—" She tried to finish the sentence through her heavy breathing.

The preacher at this moment tore off the upper part of Lily's dress, and her breasts and nipples looked out from the light into the darkness at Hobart like the troubled faces of children.

"I'm coming into the house to explain!" Hobart called to them inside.

"You'll do no such thing! No, no, Hobart!" Lily vociferated back to him, but the intruder dashed away from the window, stumbling over some low-lying bushes, and then presently entered the living room, where the preacher was now moaning deeply and beginning even at times to scream a little.

"What on earth possessed you." Lily was beginning to speak when all at once the preacher's mouth fell over hers, and he let out a great smothered roar, punctuated by drumlike rumblings from, apparently, his stomach.

Hobart took a seat near the standing couple.

The preacher was now free of Lily's body at last, and he had slumped down on the floor, near where Hobart was sitting, and was crying out some word and then he began making sounds vaguely akin to weeping. Lily remained with her back and buttocks pressed against the wall, and was breathing hard, gasping indeed for breath. After her partner had quit his peculiar sobbing, he got up and put on his clothes, and walked out unsteadily into the kitchen. On the long kitchen table, the kind of table one would expect in a large school cafeteria, Hobart, from his chair, could spy at least fifteen pies of different kinds, all "homemade" by Lily expressly for the church social which was tomorrow.

He could see the preacher sit down at the big table, and cut himself a piece of Dutch apple pie. His chewing sounds at last alerted Lily to what was happening, and she managed to hurry out to the kitchen in an attempt to halt him.

"One piece of pie isn't going to wreck the church picnic. Go back there and entertain your new boyfriend, why don't you," the preacher snapped at her attempt to prevent him eating the piece of pie.

"He's Edward Starr's brother, I'd have you know, and he's not my boyfriend, smarty!"

The preacher chewed on. "This pie," he said, moving his tongue over his lips cautiously, "is very heavy on the sugar, isn't it?"

"Oh, I declare, hear him!" Lily let the words out peevishly, and she rushed on back into the living room. There she gazed wide-eyed, her mouth trying to move for speech, for facing her stood Hobart, folding his shorts neatly, and stark naked.

"You will not!" Lily managed to protest.

"Who says I don't!" Hobart replied nastily.

"Hobart Starr, you go home at once," Lily ordered him. "This is all something that can be explained."

He made a kind of dive at her as his reply, and pinioned her to the wall. She tried to grab his penis, clawing at it, but he had perhaps already foreseen she might do this, and he caught her by the hand, and then slapped her. Then he inserted his membrum virile quickly into her body, and covered her face with his freely flowing saliva. She let out perfunctory cries of expected rather than felt pain as one does under the hand of a nervous intern.

At a motion from her, some moments later, he worked her body about the room, so that she could see what the preacher was doing. He had consumed the Dutch apple pie, and was beginning on the rhubarb lattice.

"Will you be more comfortable watching him, or shall we return to the wall?" Hobart inquired.

"Oh, Hobart, for pity's sake," she begged him. "Let me go, oh please let me go." At this he pushed himself more deeply upwards, hurting her, to judge by her grimace.

"I am a very slow comer, as you will remember, Lily. I'm slow but I'm the one in the end who cares for you most. Tonight is my biggest windfall. After all the others, you see, it is me who was meant for you. . . . You're so cozy too, Lily."

As he said this, she writhed, and attempted to pull out from him, but he kissed her hard, working into her hard.

"Oh this is all so damned unfair!" She seemed to cough out, not speak, these words. "Ralph," she directed her voice to the kitchen, "come in here and restore order. . . ."

As he reached culmination, Hobart screamed so loud the preacher did come out of the kitchen. He was swallowing very hard, so that he did remind Hobart of a man in a pie-eating contest. He looked critically at the two engaged in coitus.

A few minutes later, finished with Lily, Hobart began putting on his clothes, yawning convulsively, and shaking his head, while Ralph began doggedly and methodically to remove his clothing again, like a substitute or second in some grueling contest.

"Nothing more, no, I say no!" Lily shouted when she saw Ralph's naked body advancing on her. "I will no longer cooperate here."

He had already taken her, however, and secured her more firmly than the last time against the wall.

Hobart meanwhile was standing unsteadily on the threshold of the kitchen. He saw at once that the preacher had eaten two pies. He felt un-understandably both hungry and nauseous, and these two sensations kept him weaving giddily about the kitchen table now. At last he sat down before a chocolate meringue pie, and then very slowly, finickily, cut himself a small piece.

As he ate daintily he thought that he had not enjoyed intercourse with Lily, despite his seeming gusto. It had been all mostly exertion and effort, somehow, though he felt he had done well, but no feeling in a supreme sense of release had come. He was not surprised now that Edward Starr had left her. She was not a satisfier.

Hobart had finished about half the chocolate meringue when he reckoned the other two must be reaching culmination by now for he heard very stertorous breathing out there, and then there came to his ears as before the preacher's intense war whoop of release. Lily also screamed and appealed as if to the mountain outside, *I perish! Oh, perishing!* And a bit later, she hysterically supplicated to some unknown person or thing *I cannot give myself up like this, oh!* Then a second or so later he heard his own name called, and her demand that he save her.

Hobart wiped his mouth on the tablecloth and came out to have a look at them. They were both, Lily and Ralph, weeping and holding loosely to one another, and then they both slipped and fell to the floor, still sexually connected.

"Gosh all get out!" Hobart said with disgust.

He turned away. There was a pie at the very end of the table which looked most inviting. It had a very brown crust with golden juice spilling from fancily, formally cut little air holes as in magazine advertising. He plunged the knife into it, and tasted a tiny bit. It was of such wonderful flavor that even though he felt a bit queasy he could not resist cutting himself a slice, and he began to chew solemnly on it. It was an apricot, or perhaps peach, pie, but final identification eluded him.

Lily now came out into the kitchen and hovered over the big table. She was dressed, and had fixed her hair differently, so that it looked as if it had been cut and set, though there were some loose strands in the back which were not too becoming, yet they emphasized her white neck.

"Why, you have eaten half the pies for the church social!" she cried, with some exaggeration in her observation, of course. "After all that backbreaking work of mine! What on earth will I tell the preacher when he comes to pick them up!"

"But isn't this the preacher here tonight?" Hobart waving his fork in the direction of the other room motioned to the man called Ralph.

"Why, Hobart, of course not. . . . He's no preacher, and I should think you could tell . . ."

"How did I come to think he was?" Hobart stuttered out, while Lily sat down at the table and was beginning to bawl.

"Of all the inconsiderate selfish thoughtless pups in the world," she managed to get out between sobs. "I would have to meet up with you two, just when I was beginning to have some sort of settled purpose."

Ralph, standing now on the threshold of the kitchen, still stark naked, laughed.

"I have a good notion to call the sheriff!" Lily threatened. "And do you know what I'm going to do in the morning? I'm going back to Edward Starr in Chicago. Yes siree. I realize now that he loved me more than I was aware of at the time."

The two men were silent, and looked cautiously at one another, while Lily cried on and on.

"Oh, Lily," Hobart said, "even if you do go see Edward, you'll come home again to us here. You know you can't get the good loving in Chicago that we give you, now don't you?"

Lily wept on and on repeating many times how she would never be able to explain to the church people about not having enough pies on hand for her contribution to the big social.

After drying her tears on a handkerchief which Hobart lent her, she took the knife and with methodical fierce energy and spiteful speed cut herself a serving from one of the still-untouched pies.

She showed by the way she moved her tongue in and out of her mouth that she thought her piece was excellent.

"I'm going to Chicago and I'm never coming back!" As she delivered this statement she began to cry again.

The "preacher," for that is how Hobart still thought of him, came over to where Lily was chewing and weeping, and put his hand between the hollow of her breasts.

"Now don't get started again, Ralph. . . . No!" she flared up. "No, no, no."

"I need it all over again," Ralph appealed to her. "Your good cooking has charged me up again."

"Those pies *are* too damned good for a church," she finally said with a sort of moody weird craftiness, and Ralph knew when she said this that she would let him have her again.

"Hobart"—Lily turned to Edward's brother—"why don't you go home. Ralph and I are old childhood friends from way back. And I was nice to you. But I am in love with Ralph."

"It's my turn," Hobart protested.

"No, no." Lily began her weeping again. "I love Ralph."

"Oh hell, let him just this once more, Lily," the "preacher" said. Ralph walked away and began toying again with another of the uncut pies. "Say, who taught you to cook, Lily?" he inquired sleepily.

"I want you to send Hobart home, Ralph. I want you to myself. In a bed. This wall stuff is an outrage. Ralph, you send Hobart home now."

"Oh why don't you let the fellow have you once more. Then I'll really do you upstairs." Meanwhile, he went on chewing and swallowing loudly.

"Damn you, Ralph," Lily moaned. "Double damn you."

She walked over to the big table and took up one of the pies nearest her and threw it straight at the "preacher."

The "preacher" 's eyes, looking out from the mess she had made of his face, truly frightened her. She went over to Hobart, and waited there.

"All right for you, Lily," the "preacher" said.

"Oh, don't hurt her," Hobart pleaded, frightened too at the "preacher" 's changed demeanor.

The first pie the "preacher" threw hit Hobart instead of Lily. He let out a little gasp, more perhaps of surprised pleasure than hurt.

"Oh now stop this. We must stop this," Lily exhorted. "We are grown-up people, after all." She began to sob, but very put-on like, the men felt. "Look at my kitchen." She tried to put some emphasis into her appeal to them.

The "preacher" took off his jockey shorts, which he had put on a few moments earlier. He took first one pie and then another, mashing them all over his body, including his hair. Lily began to whimper and weep in earnest now, and sat down as if to give herself over to her grief. Suddenly one of the pies hit her, and she began to scream, then she became silent.

There was a queer silence in the whole room. When she looked up, Hobart had also stripped completely, and the "preacher" was softly slowly mashing pies over his thin, tightly muscled torso. Then slowly, inexorably, Hobart began eating pieces of pie from off the body of the smeared "preacher." The "preacher" returned this favor, and ate pieces of pie from Hobart, making gobbling sounds like a wild animal. Then they hugged one another and began eating the pies all over again from their bare bodies.

"Where do you get that stuff in my house!" Lily rose, roaring at them. "You low curs, where do you—"

But the "preacher" had thrown one of the few remaining pies at her, which struck her squarely in the breast and blew itself red all over her face and body so that she resembled a person struck by a bomb.

Ralph hugged Hobart very tenderly now, and dutifully ate small tidbits from his body, and Hobart seemed to nestle against Ralph's body, and ate selected various pieces of the pie from the latter.

Then Lily ran out the front door and began screaming *Help! I will perish! Help me!*

The dogs began to bark violently all around the neighborhood.

In just a short time she returned. The two men were still closely together, eating a piece here and there from their "massacred" bodies.

Sitting down at the table, weeping perfunctorily and almost inaudibly, Lily raised her fork, and began eating a piece of her still-unfinished apple pie.

On the Rebound

"Frankly, gentlemen," Rupert Douthwaite reflected one gray afternoon in January to a few of us Americans who visited him from time to time in his "exile" in London, "no one in New York, no one who counted, ever expected to see Georgia Comstock back in town," and here Rupert nodded on the name, in his coy, pompous but somewhat charming way, meaning for us to know she was an heiress, meaning she had "everything," otherwise he would not be mentioning her. "She sat right there." He pointed to a refurbished heirloom chair which had accompanied him from New York. "I would never have dreamed Georgia would sue for a favor, least of all to me, for, after all"—he touched a colorful sideburn—"if you will allow me to remind you, it was I who replaced Georgia so far as literary salons were concerned." He groaned heavily, one of his old affectations, and took out his monocle, one of his new ones, and let it rest on the palm of his hand like an expiring butterfly. "Georgia's was, after all, the only bona fide salon in New York for years and years—I say that, kind friends, without modification. It was never elegant, never grand, never *comme il faut,* granted, any more than poor Georgia was. She was plain, mean, and devastating, with her own consistent vulgarity and bad taste, but she had the energy of a fiend out of hot oil and she turned that energy into establishing the one place where everybody had to turn up on a Thursday in New York, whether he liked it or not.

"When the dear thing arrived, then, at my place after her long banishment, I was pained to see how much younger she'd gotten. It didn't become her. I preferred her old, let's say. It was obvious she'd had the finest face-lifting job Europe can bestow. (You know how they've gone all wrong in New York on that. You remember Kathryn Combs, the film beauty. One eye's higher than the other now, dead mouth, and so on, so that I always feel when Kathryn's about I'm looking into an open casket.) But Georgia! Well, she hardly looked forty.

"Now mind you, I knew she hadn't come back to New York to tell me she loved me—the woman's probably hated me all my life, no doubt about it, but whatever she'd come for, I had to remind myself she had been helpful when Kitty left me." Rupert referred openly now to his third wife, the great New York female novelist who had walked out on him for, in his words, a shabby little colonel. "Yes," he sighed now, "when all the papers were full of my divorce before I myself hardly knew she had left me, Georgia was most understanding, even kind, moved in to take care of me, hovered over me like a mother bird, and so on. I had been ready to jump in the river, and she, bitch that she is, brought me round. And so when she appeared five years to the day after New York had kicked her out, and with her brand-new face, I saw at once she had come on a matter as crucial to her as my bust-up had been with Kitty, but I confess I never dreamed she had come to me because she wanted to begin all over again (begin with a salon, I mean of course). Nobody decent begins again, as I tried to tell her immediately I heard what she was up to. She'd been living in Yugoslavia, you know, after the New York fiasco. . . .

"When she said she did indeed want to begin again, I simply replied, 'Georgia, you're not serious and you're not as young as you look either, precious. You can't know what you're saying. Maybe it's the bad New York air that's got you after the wheat fields and haymows of Slavonia.'

" 'Rupert, my angel,' she intoned, 'I'm on my knees to you, and not rueful to be so! Help me to get back and to stay back, dearest!'

" 'Nonsense'—I made her stop her dramatics—'I won't hear of it, and you won't hear of it either when you're yourself again.'

"I was more upset than I should have been, somehow. Her coming and her wish for another try at a salon made me aware what was already in the wind, something wicked that scared me a little, and I heard myself voicing it when I said, 'Everything has changed in New York, sweety, since you've been away. You wouldn't know anybody now. Most of the old writers are too afraid to go out even for a stroll anymore, and the new ones, you see, meet only on the parade ground. The salon, dear love, I'm afraid, is through.'

" 'I feel I can begin again, Rupert, darling.' She ignored my speech. 'You know it was everything to me, it's everything now. Don't speak to me of the Yugoslav pure air and haymows.'

"Well, I looked her up and down, and thought about every-thing. There she was, worth twenty million she'd inherited from her pa's death, and worth another six or seven million from what the movies gave her for her detective novels, for Georgia was, whether you boys remember or not, a novelist in her own right. Yet here she was, a flood of grief. I've never seen a woman want anything so much, and in my day I've seen them with their tongues hanging for just about everything.

" 'Let me fix you a nice tall frosty drink like they don't have in Zagreb, angel, and then I'm going to bundle you up and send you home to bed.' But she wouldn't be serious. 'Rupert, my love, if as you said I saved you once '(she overstated, of course),' you've got to save me now.'

"She had come to the heart of her mission.

" 'What did I do wrong before, will you tell me,' she brought out after a brief struggle with pride. 'Why was I driven out of New York, my dear boy. Why was I blacklisted, why was every door slammed in my face.' She gave a short sob.

" 'Georgia, my sweet, if you don't know why you had to leave New York, nobody can tell you.' I was a bit abrupt.

" 'But I don't, Rupert!' She was passionate. 'Cross my heart,' she moaned. 'I don't.'

"I shook my finger at her.

" 'You sit there, dear Douthwaite, like the appointed monarch of all creation whose only burden is to say no to all mortal pleas.' She laughed a little, then added, 'Don't be needlessly cruel, you beautiful thing.'

" 'I've never been that,' I told her. 'Not cruel. But, Georgia, you know what you did, and said, the night of your big fiasco, after which oblivion moved in on you. You burned every bridge, highway, and cowpath behind you when you attacked the Negro novelist Burleigh Jordan in front of everybody who matters on the literary scene.'

" 'I? Attacked him?' she scoffed.

" 'My God, you can't pretend you don't remember.' I studied her new mouth and chin. 'Burleigh's grown to even greater importance since *you* left, Georgia. First he was the greatest black writer, then he was the greatest Black, and, now, God knows what he is, I've not kept hourly track. But when you insulted him that night, though your ruin was already in the air, it was the end for you, and nearly the end for all of us. I had immediately to go to work to salvage my own future.'

" 'Ever the master of overstatement, dear boy,' she sighed.

"But I was stony-faced.

" 'So you mean what you say?' she whined, after daubing an eye.

" 'I mean only this, Georgia,' I said, emphasizing the point in question. 'I took over when you destroyed yourself' (and I waited to let it sink in that my own salon, which had been so tiny when Georgia's had been so big, had been burgeoning while she was away, and had now more than replaced her. I was *her* now, in a manner of speaking).

" 'Supposing then you tell me straight out what I said to Burleigh.' She had turned her back on me while she examined a new painting I had acquired, as a matter of fact, only a day or so before. I could tell she didn't think much of it, for she turned from it almost at once.

" 'Well?' she prompted me.

" 'Oh, don't expect me to repeat your exact words after all the water has flowed under the bridge since you said them. Your words were barbarous, of course, but it was your well-known tone of voice, as well as the exquisitely snotty timing of what you said, that did the trick. You are the empress of all bitches, darling, and if you wrote books as stabbing as you talk, you'd have no peer. . . . You said in four or five different rephrasings of your original affidavit that you would never kiss a black ass if it meant you and your Thursdays were to be ground to powder.'

" 'Oh, I completely disremember such a droll statement.' She giggled.

"Just then the doorbell rang, and in came four or five eminent writers, all of whom were surprised to see Georgia, and Georgia could not mask her own surprise that they were calling on me so casually. We rather ignored her then, but she wouldn't leave, and when they found the bottles and things, and were chattering away, Georgia pushed herself among us, and began on me again.

"At last more to get rid of her than anything else, I proposed to her the diabolic, unfeasible scheme which I claimed would reinstate her everywhere, pave the way for the reopening of her Thursday salon. I am called everywhere the most soulless cynic who ever lived, but I swear by whatever any of you hold holy, if you ever hold anything, that I never dreamed she would take me on when I said to her that all she'd be required to do was give Burleigh the token kiss she'd said she never would, to make it formal and she'd be back in business. You see, I thought she would leave in a huff when she heard my innocent proposal and that in a few days New York would see her no more—at least I'd be rid of her. Well, say she'd quaffed one too many of my frosty masterpieces, say again it was the poisonous New York air, whatever, I stood dumbfounded when I heard her say simply, 'Then make it next Thursday, darling, and I'll be here, and tell Burleigh not to fail us, for I'll do it, Rupert, darling, I'll do it for you, I'll do it for all of us.'

"The next day I rang to tell her of course that she wasn't to take me seriously, that my scheme had been mere persiflage, etc. She simply rang off after having assured me the deal was on and she'd be there Thursday.

"I was so angry with the bitch by then I rang up big black Burleigh and simply, without a word of preparation, told him. You see, Burleigh and I were more than friends at that time, let's put it that way." Rupert smirked a bit with his old self-assurance. "And," he went on, "to my mild surprise, perhaps, the dear lion agreed to the whole thing with alacrity.

"After a few hours of sober reflection, I panicked. I called Burleigh back first and tried to get him not to come. But Burleigh was at the height of a new wave of paranoia and idol worship and he could do no wrong. He assured me he wanted to come, wanted to go through with our scheme, which he baptized divine. I little knew then, of course, how well he had planned to go through with it, and neither, of course, did poor Georgia!

"Then, of course, I tried again to get Georgia not to come. It was like persuading Joan of Arc to go back to her livestock. I saw everything coming then the way it did come, well, not *everything.*" Here he looked wistfully around at the London backdrop and grinned, for he missed New York even more when he talked about it, and he hadn't even the makings of a salon in London, of course, though he'd made a stab at it.

"I didn't sleep the night before." Rupert Douthwaite went on to describe the event to which he owed his ruin. "I thought I was daring, I thought I had always been in advance of everything— after all, *my* Thursdays had been at least a generation ahead of Georgia's in smartness, taste, and éclat, and now, well, as I scented the fume-heavy air, somebody was about to take the lead over from me.

"Everybody came that night—wouldn't you know it, some people from Washington, a tiresome princess or so, and indeed all the crowned heads from all the avenues of endeavor managed to get there, as if they sensed what was to come off. There was even that fat man from Kansas City who got himself circumcised a few seasons back to make the literary scene in New York.

"Nobody recognized Georgia at first when she made her entrance, not even Burleigh. She was radiant, if slightly drawn, and for the first time I saw that her face-lifting job wasn't quite stressproof, but still she only looked half her age, and so she was a howling success at first blush.

" 'Now, my lovely'—I spoke right into her ear redolent of two-hundred-dollar-an-ounce attar of something—'please bow to everybody and then go home—my car is downstairs parked directly by the door, Wilson is at the wheel. You've made a grand hit tonight, and go now while they're all still cheering.'

" 'I'm going through with it, love.' She was adamant, and I saw Burleigh catch the old thing's eye and wink.

" 'Not in my house, you won't,' I whispered to her, kissing her again and again in deadly desperation to disguise my murderous expression from the invited guests. 'After all,' I repeated, 'my little scheme was proposed while we were both in our cups.'

" 'And it's in cups where the truth resides, Douthwaite, as the Latin proverb has it,' and she kissed me on the lips and left me, walking around the room as in her old salon grandeur days, grasping everybody's outstretched hand, letting herself be embraced and kissed. She was a stunning, dizzy success, and then suddenly I felt that neither she nor Burleigh had any intention of doing what they had agreed to do. I was the fool who had fallen for their trap.

"When I saw what a hit she was making, I took too many drinks, for the more accolades she got, the angrier and more disturbed I became. I wasn't going to let Georgia come back and replace me, whatever else might happen.

"I went over to where Burleigh was being worshipped to death. He turned immediately to me to say, 'Don't you come over here, Ruppie, to ask me again not to do what I am sure as greased lightning I'm going to do, baby,' and he smiled his angry smile at me.

" 'Burleigh, dearest'—I took him by the hand—'I not only want you to go through with it bigger and grander but megatons more colossal than we had planned. That's the message I have to give you,' and I kissed and hugged him quietly.

"I couldn't be frightened now, and what I had just proposed to him was a little incredible even for me, even for me drunk, I had gone all out, I dimly realized, and asked for an assassination.

"But the more I saw Georgia's success with everybody, the more I wanted the horror that was going to happen. And then there was the size of her diamond. It was too much. No one wore diamonds that big in the set we moved in. She did it to hurt me, to show me up to the others, that whereas I might scrape up a million, let's say, she had so much money she couldn't add it all up short of two years of auditing.

"Time passed. I looked in the toilet where Burleigh was getting ready, and hugged encouragement.

"Then I felt the great calm people are said to feel on learning they have but six months to live. I gave up, got the easiest seat and the one nearest to the stage, and collapsed. People forgot me.

"Still the hog of the scene, Georgia was moving right to where she knew she was to give her comeback performance.

"Some last-minute celebrities had just come in, to whom I could only barely nod, a duchess, and some minor nobility, a senator, a diva, and somehow from somewhere a popular film critic of the hour who had discovered he was not homosexual, when with a boom and a guffaw Burleigh sails out of the john wearing feathers on his head but otherwise not a stitch on him.

"I saw Georgia freeze ever so slightly—you see, in our original scheme nothing was said about nakedness, it was all, in any case, to have been a token gesture, she had thought—indeed I had thought, but she stopped, put down her glass, squared her shoulders like a good soldier, and waited.

"Burleigh jumped up on my fine old walnut table cleared for the occasion. Everybody pretended to like it. Georgia began to weave around like a rabbit facing a python. Burleigh turned his back to her, and bent over, and with a war whoop extended his black biscuits to her. She stood reeling, waiting for the long count, then I heard, rather than saw, owing to heads in the way, her kissing his behind, then rising I managed to see him proffer his front and middle to her, everything there waving, when someone blotted out my view again, but I gathered from the murmur of the crowd she had gone through with it, and kissed his front too.

"Then I heard her scream, and I got up in time to see that

Burleigh had smeared her face with some black tarlike substance and left a few of his white turkey feathers over that.

"I believe Georgia tried to pretend she had wanted this last too, and that it was all a grand charade, but her screams belied it, and she and Burleigh stood facing one another like victims of a car accident.

"It had all failed, I realized immediately. Everybody was sickened or bored. Nothing was a success about it. Call it wrong timing, wrong people, wrong actors or hour of the evening, oh explain it any way you will, it was all ghastly and cruddy with nonsuccess.

"I stumbled over to the back of my apartment, and feeling queasy, lay down on the floor near the rubber plant. I thought queerly of Kitty, who had, it seemed, just left me, and I—old novelist *manqué*—thought of all those novels I had written which publishers never even finished reading in typescript, let alone promised to publish, and I gagged loudly. People bent down to me and seemed to take my pulse, and then others began filing out, excusing themselves by a cough or nod, or stifling a feeble giggle. They thought I had fainted from chagrin. They thought I had not planned it. They thought I was innocent but ruined.

"I have never seen such a clean, wholesale, bloody failure. Like serving a thin, warm soup and calling it baked Alaska.

"I didn't see anybody for weeks. Georgia, I understand, left for Prague a few days later. Only Burleigh was not touched by anything. Nothing can harm him, bad reviews, public derision, all he has to do is clap his hands, and crowds hoist him on their shoulders, the money falls like rain in autumn.

"Burleigh has his own salon now, if you can call his big gatherings on Saturday a salon, and Georgia and I both belong to a past more remote than the French and Indian Wars.

"To answer your first question, Gordon"—Rupert turned now

to me, for I was his favorite American of the moment—"I've found London quieting, yes, but it's not my world exactly, sweety, since I'm not in or of it, but that's what I need, isn't it, to sit on the sidelines for a season and enjoy a statelier backdrop? I don't quite know where Georgia is. Somebody says it's Bulgaria."

Ruthanna Elder

Dr. Ulric laid much of his insomnia to the fact that he had too meticulous a memory of the subsequent lives of the more than two thousand babies he had delivered in his time. Their histories weighed on him sometimes as heavy as the slabs from the stone quarry.

Dr. Ulric, aged seventy-five, went for a short walk, then encouraged by the mild evening air he passed beyond the confines of the cornfield surrounding his property, and soon stood before an empty frame house with an enormous door, boarded up, frowning at him in the half-light. It seemed, in the outworn phrase, indeed only yesterday that Ruthanna Elder, the one-time occupant of the house, had spoken with the doctor. Charles Ulric returned home then, but all that night, as he moved his head from one pillow to another in his struggle with his enemy sleeplessness, Ruthanna's story kept presenting itself to him like the streamers of northern lights in the autumn sky.

Ruthanna Elder, who had died only last year, had been the

prom queen of such and such a year, and after the blow which life had given her at the age of seventeen, she had sat out the next few years on the very front porch in front of the door which tonight had bestowed on Dr. Ulric his sleeplessness. Until only last spring, Ruthanna, slightly bowed from remaining for too long in a sitting position, but looking younger than many of this year's high school graduates, held her head in a way that suggested she still wore the crown of her brief reign.

Dr. Ulric deep in wakefulness remembered now still further back to that afternoon before the graduation ball when Ruthanna had cautiously entered his office where he had delivered babies, removed bullets from wounded men, set bones, pronounced men dead.

"No, Ruthanna, you are not pregnant." The doctor felt he heard his own voice in the country stillness. "But if you worry so, my dear, why don't you marry your young man, Jess Ference, since you're both graduating in a little while. . . . Get married, if you're that worried."

Ruthanna had cried then a lot, but had finally managed to say, "It was not Jess Ference, Doctor. . . . That is why I have been so worried."

"Did you want to tell me then who it was?" the doctor inquired after he had let her cry out more of her grief. She was in no mood to leave.

"It was my uncle, Dr. Ulric." She gave out the secret which troubled her so ceaselessly. "He approached me after he had invited me to his folks' new house where you can see where the river carried off the bridge in the big flood of two years ago. . . ."

Unlike most uncles, the doctor mused, this uncle was two years younger than she, making him fifteen.

The uncle had closed and then locked the door, Ruthanna remembered silently as the doctor watched her uneasily.

"But don't you see, dear," Dr. Ulric had spoken over her thoughts, "you are not going to have a baby. . . . My examination, Ruthanna, has proved that. You did not conceive," he went on to her incredulous face, "from your uncle's being with you. . . . You'll be fine for Jess Ference. . . ."

"But why, Doctor, then, can't I seem to give Jess my promise for our wedding day? When it is after all Jess that I have loved since we were children. . . . But no, I cannot, the words stick in my throat. . . ."

"But have you really tried to tell Jess you love him and wish to be married to him?"

"Oh, yes, I think so. . . . But as I say . . . the words stick. It is as if my uncle held my tongue. . . ."

"That is wrong." Dr. Ulric was severe. "You must tell Jess you are free to marry him. And you need not give away what happened with a blood relation. Tell Jess yes. Or tell him no. But you must not vacillate. . . . He loves you too dearly!"

At the graduation ball, Jess's face had blurred as Ruthanna felt him hold her, and she could only see and remember the uncle closing and then locking the door. . . . She loved Jess with all her heart, but why could she think of nothing but the *closed door.*

Her uncle had removed her blouse, and placed his young lips on her untouched breasts. She had melted under his arms like the river freed from ice.

Jess had looked hurt as he had danced with her that night. He had looked like a man who has been slapped with a wet towel. He had always feared from boyhood there might be someone else, but now he was sure.

But there was nobody, of course, her uncle was not Ruthanna's love, her uncle had only taken her, he was not a real uncle after all but a boy, almost a child, although still the first out of all the ones who had wanted her, had waited for her, and who had first possessed her.

Jess had walked away from the dance like a man in a dream to the young uncle's house, the music drifting away now in the distance, for a chance word from somebody had kindled his suspicion into flame.

He had waked the boy after midnight. Jess had asked him if it was true he had loved Ruthanna. The young man, still in the enclosure of sleep, had not denied anything, he had added indeed all the missing or wanted details. It was the details that had done their terrible work, people later said. Had the uncle only told the fiancé *yes* and then said no more what happened later would never have happened.

But the uncle had told it all so lovingly as if he were confiding to a kind brother, a brother whom he loved as much as he had loved Ruthanna. He held Jess's hand in his as he talked, he wept and told him everything, he touched his face to Jess's cheeks, wetting them also and perhaps he added details which were not precisely consonant with the truth in order to satisfy his late visitor.

Jess had stumbled out of the uncle's house at about daybreak. He had walked down to the stone quarry, past Five Creeks, and beyond the glue factory to where the river glided slow and not too deep this time of year. Then he went back to his own house, and got the gun.

Ruthanna had been promised to Jess since he was a boy. It was arranged, you see, their marriage from the "beginning," from, it seemed to Jess at that moment, before their birth.

The young uncle was seated at breakfast, his eyes riveted on the comic section of the Sunday papers.

Jess had walked up to him with a strange smile ruffling his mouth.

The uncle looked up, turned his untroubled gaze and brow toward his assassin-to-be. He had no chance to beg for pardon. Jess shot once, then twice, the bowl of morning cereal was covered with red like a dish of fresh-gathered berries.

Jess walked out with comely carriage to Ruthanna's house. He stood before the white pillars and fired the same gun into his head, his brains and pieces of skull rushed out from under his fair curly hair onto the glass behind the pillars, onto the screen door, the blood flew like a gentle summer shower. Jess Ference lay on the front steps, the veins in his outstretched hands swollen as if they still carried blood to his stilled heart.

Sleep Tight

Little Judd was about five years old when his sister Nelle mentioned the Sandman to him. Up until that time he had talked and thought mostly about fire chiefs, policemen, soldiers, and of course sailors, because his daddy had gone to sea.

" 'Your daddy is sailing the ocean wide,' " Sister Nelle would sing in a fruitless endeavor to get him to sleep. But that was the one thing little Judd could not do. About dawn he slumbered for a few hours, but during the night, almost never.

Then in despair Nelle had thought of the Sandman and told Judd he would come and put him to sleep if the boy would get quiet and promise not to turn on the radio or play with his watercolors and stain the bedclothes.

"Sandman will come and make your eyelids heavy," Nelle had promised him. "But only if you will be good and lie quiet and still in your bed."

Then Nelle would sing him another song, this last one about

the red red robin who comes bob-bob-bobbing along, and Judd
would grin when he heard the familiar words.

"Sing more about the robin, why don't you," he coaxed her.

Nelle would sing until she was hoarse, but it only made Judd
more wakeful.

~·~·~·~·~

"There is no end to your repertory of songs, Nelle, I declare!"
their mother said one evening after Nelle had come downstairs
exhausted and pale from trying to put him to sleep.

"I should never have told him about the Sandman," Nelle
confessed. "Now he keeps awake on purpose to meet him."

"Don't blame yourself, Nelle, where he is concerned," Mother
comforted her. "Whatever we do with regard to little Judd is
bound to go wrong." She sighed and took off her apron, folded
it, and laid it in the dirty-clothes basket.

Little Judd, as a matter of fact, had thought of almost nothing but the Sandman since Nelle had mentioned him. Yet no
matter how much he had questioned his sister about him, Nelle
had been unable either to describe his appearance or explain
exactly how he was able to put the grains of sand on boys' eyelids. Also, little Judd had wanted to know what sort of a box or
sack the Sandman kept his sand in. Nelle was such poor help in
filling out these details that the boy became much more wakeful
than ever.

~·~·~·~·~

One night long after his mother and Nelle had gone to sleep
downstairs, little Judd heard a strange noise. Turning round, he
was sure he was looking right at the Sandman himself, who had
crawled in through his open window. He was a tall dark man
wearing a sort of Halloween mask, and he had long blue gloves
on. There was a large red wet spot on his chest.

He was breathing heavily and every so often he would double all up and hold his belly and say, "Owww."

"Sandman?" little Judd inquired.

The dark man with the mask stared cautiously now at the boy while continuing to make his "Oww" sounds.

"Come on now, mister, give me some of your sand, why don't you!"

The man hesitated for a moment, then came noiselessly over to the boy and sat down heavily on the bed beside him.

"Did you come tonight specially for me?" the boy wondered.

"Yes." The man spoke after brief hesitation. "You can say that, I suppose." He smiled ever so little and began to touch the boy's shoulder, then stopped.

"You're sure you are him, though?" Judd spoke earnestly and loudly.

The Sandman nodded weakly in response, put his finger to his lips and whispered *Shhh*.

"Why don't you give little Judd then some of your sand?" the boy also whispered.

The Sandman started to reply but was halted abruptly by the blaring sound of police sirens outside. His eyes closed and opened nervously as if to convey the rest of his explanation.

But little Judd, who hated the long silence of the night, clapped his hands for joy at the tumult outside. He loved anything that broke the terrible quiet in which he was always tossing and turning and wondering where his father was as he sailed over the shoreless sea.

"I'll give you some sand, little Judd," the visitor spoke out now, "if you'll promise not to tell anybody I am here." Saying this, he stood up with difficulty. "Remember, though, if they ask you whether anybody paid you a call tonight, tell them *only the Sandman*. Hear? Now we'll see about giving you quite a little pile of sand. . . ."

"What is wrong with your chest, Sandman?" Judd questioned, staring at the stranger more closely. All of a sudden, little Judd took the man's hand in his. Then after holding it tightly for a bit, he cried, "Why, see what you have did to my blanket! It looks like you had spilled my red watercolor paints all over it."

The visitor bent over lazily, and his half-opened lips touched briefly the boy's soft yellow hair.

"Now then, little Judd," the man began when he saw how calm the boy had become in his presence. "I will go into that clothes closet over yonder, you see, and I will get you some grains of sand. While I am a-getting them, though, don't you tell nobody at all I am here, dig?"

His eyes fell to where his hand was imprisoned by the boy's grasp. Quickly pulling his hand free, he walked to the closet and opened the door. Turning about to little Judd, he whispered in the softest tone yet, "I will go get you your sand now, Judd."

Below, the front door bell was ringing in alarm, and Judd could hear over that sound his mother calling out, *"All right, all right,"* in the same loud provoked voice she used after he had wet the bed and she would cry, *"We can't keep you in rubber pants, can we, I declare!"*

"Yes, Officer." His mother's voice drifted up to him while he kept his eyes fixed on the closet door.

"No, we haven't heard a thing, have we, Nelle?" Mother went on in a soaring, scared voice.

Presently Judd heard footsteps scurrying up the stairs and in no time at all Sister Nelle was peeking through the half-opened door. Meantime, outside, the whole neighborhood had come awake. More sirens and police whistles shattered the air.

"What is it, Nelle?" Judd spoke slyly, still keeping his eyes on the closet door.

Nelle studied him carefully. "There's been a robbery," she began, but then stopped and looked suspiciously around the room.

"Someone got shot," she said in a very low voice. "Anyhow, you had best go back to sleep, dear. . . . It's all over." She seemed queer as she spoke, and her eye roved unsatisfied about the room.

Before she could go down again, heavy unfamiliar footsteps reverberated over the threadbare stair treads.

A great man dressed in a blue uniform stood at the door, behind whom, looking white and little, was Mother.

"Everything seems to be all right in here," the police sergeant announced, as if to the room itself. He crossed the threshold and his hand rested for a moment over the hinge of the closet door.

The sergeant smiled then at Judd. "You hear anything, sonny?"

"Just the Sandman," Judd replied in his accustomed sharp tone of voice. Nelle smiled embarrassedly at his reply.

The sergeant and Mother left the room.

"We can't be too careful, Mrs. Bond." The sergeant's voice came to Judd's ears as strong and loud as when he had stood by the closet door. "We'd like to search the yard again and the basement."

Judd heard his mother crying then; Nelle went out into the hall, and her footsteps could soon be heard retreating downstairs. More sirens screamed, coming very close to home, and a man called something through a bullhorn.

"You can come out, Sandman," Judd whispered. There was no answer from the closet.

"Sandman," Judd whispered a little louder. "Come out, and give me some sand. I want to go to sleep. Please . . . pretty please!"

The upstairs was quiet now, but he could hear people moving about down below, and the sergeant was saying something comforting to Mother.

"You needn't be afraid, Mrs. Bond. He is probably a long way from here by now. . . . And our detail will remain here throughout the night. . . ."

Nelle's voice now rose up too: "It's all right, Mother. . . . Please don't cry so hard. . . ."

"Sandman," Judd said out loud.

Just as he spoke, the closet door came open wide, and the Sandman stared, rigid, into the room, but not really looking in the direction of the boy. The wet red circle on his chest had grown larger and covered almost all of his shirt. His eyes looked different also, like little bonfires about to go out.

All at once the Sandman pitched forward, and then, as if trying to break his fall, he twisted and landed face up on the floor.

"What on earth was that noise?" Mother cried from her chair in the kitchen. "My God, don't tell me . . ."

Judd stepped over the Sandman, hurried to the door, opened it, and called down, "It's all right, Mama. I upset the big chair."

"All right, dearest," Mother replied, forgetting to correct him for being awake. "I will be up to see you presently."

Little Judd was the happiest he had been since the day he and his daddy had played Grizzly Bear together. His dad had imitated a fierce bear and then just before he was going to bite him, little Judd had shot his daddy with a toy BB gun, and he had fallen down and lain very still.

Little Judd now went into the closet where the Sandman had been hiding and got his toy gun. He shot the Sandman four or five times. But the Sandman did not play right, as his daddy had. Instead he made strange sounds, which were not too pleasant, and a kind of pink foam formed on his lips, which had never happened with his dad.

Little Judd saw also that the Sandman was very black, and indeed he had never set eyes on anybody that dark except once when a parade had gone by near his house and a large file of dark men and women had shouted and screamed and waved flags.

"Where is the sand you promised me?" little Judd complained.

He looked at the nozzle of his gun and then studied the way the red wet spot on the Sandman's chest kept growing still larger. It was summer and the visitor had very little on except his thin stained shirt and his blue trousers. His feet were naked.

He decided the Sandman had been playing with his watercolors in the closet, which explained the red, or was it he had shot the Sandman so hard he had hurt him with his gun? Whatever it was, it made him want to do watercolors with the wet red that was coming from the Sandman.

"Judd?" he heard his mother's voice from below. "Judd, darling?"

He hurried to the door, opened it softly, and called down *Yes* to her.

"You're sure you're all right, precious?" Judd made kissing sounds in reply and then said, cupping his hands so perhaps only his mother would hear him, "The Sandman has been here."

He heard his mother laugh and put her coffee cup down with a bang.

Behind the closed door, little Judd made a drawing on his watercolor paper of a ship at sea and a sailor looking at the rough waves.

There was so much watercolor red, though, that his paint box was suddenly flooded with it. It was the best watercolor he had ever used, thick and yet runny. No wonder Nelle had talked so much about the Sandman if he brought such good colors to paint with.

After a while, though, little Judd got tired. He had used up all his paper, and then, too, he noticed that the Sandman wasn't making any more paint. Only from his mouth did a kind of pink something issue, but finally that stopped too.

"Sandman, it's time for you to leave. The day is coming, and nobody wants your sand in the sunlight." Little Judd was looking at the orange light streaming through the window. "Sandman, go home," he repeated. "Come back when it's dark and bring me a different color for my paintbrush. . . ."

Little Judd yawned.

It had been an unusual night, he knew, but something was not unusual: he had not slept a wink.

This began to puzzle him, for here the Sandman himself had spent all night with him, and all he had given him was red watercolors.

Again, as so often in the past, Judd felt very sleepy now that day was actually coming. But his bed was too wet with the Sandman's red watercolors.

There was a strong strange smell in the room now, and large black flies had flown in the open window and come to rest on the face and chest of the Sandman. They buzzed and moved their feet in a slithery way, rose in the air, then alighted again on the quiet Sandman.

The buzzing of the flies and the strange sweet smell in the bedroom made little Judd uncomfortable. He felt he was going to be sick. He whimpered a little.

Then he began to realize that he had made a mistake, or Sister Nelle had not told him the exact truth. That is, the black man who lay there so still with the flies swarming on his mouth and chest was perhaps not a real Sandman, for if he was the Sandman, Judd surely would have slept, and he would not have had red watercolors bestowed on him but golden grains of sand.

Then he began to cry very loud. He screamed finally, as he had when he wet his rubber pants.

At last he heard Nelle's step outside the door.

"What is it now, little Judd?" He heard her voice against the closed door.

"I have shot and killed the Sandman," little Judd replied.

"He's all covered with watercolors and flies, and I have killed him."

"You try to get some sleep now." Nelle still spoke through the wood of the door. "It's only five-thirty in the morning. . . . Use the potty under your bed if you have to, little Judd."

"I thought he was the Sandman, but I guess he ain't." Little Judd went on speaking to his sister. "I shot him to death with my gun, I guess."

"Use the potty if you can," Nelle told him. Her voice sounded as sleepy as if she had dozed off leaning on the closed door.

"Shall I come in and help you, Judd?"

There was no reply.

"Little Judd!" Nelle cried.

It was then that Sister Nelle opened the door. She stood a long time staring first at the dead man on the floor, then at little Judd, then at the bloodstains on the floor, and all over the many sheets of the watercolor paper. Then Nelle began to scream, at first a low scream, then a more prolonged louder one, and at last, from her astonished countenance, many piercing cries that recalled sirens and bullhorn. Little Judd screamed in response, as if they were singing to one another, echoing one another, as they did together with the red red robin.

Short Papa

When I caught a glimpse of Short Papa coming through the backyard that cold, sleety February afternoon I had straight away a funny feeling it might be the last time he would visit me. He looked about the same, tall and lean and wind-burned, but despite the way he kept his shoulders back and his head up he spoke and shook hands like a man who didn't expect you to believe a word he said.

Neither Mama nor Sister Ruth budged an inch when I told them who was out on the back porch, but after a struggle with herself, Ma finally said, "You can give Short Papa this plate of hot Brunswick stew, and let him get his strength back from wherever he has been this time. And then you tell him, Lester, he has got to light out again soon as possible."

"But, Ma," I began, "can't he stay just the night?"

"Father or no father," she began, "after what that man has done to us, no . . . I'll feed him but I won't take him in, and you give him my message, hear? Eat and get!"

But I seen that my remark about how after all it was my own dad who had come to see me had moved Ma more than a little, for her breast rose and fell like it always does when she is wrought up.

"He'll only get in more trouble if he stays, Lester, and he'll get you in trouble too. I do regret to talk against your papa, but he is a no-account, low-down . . ."

She stopped, though, when she saw the expression on my face.

Short Papa sat, hands folded, on a little green wicker upright chair before the round green wicker table as I brought him his hot plate of Brunswick stew to the back porch.

"Thank you, Les." He eyed the plate and then took it from me. I can still see the way he ate the fricassee chicken and little bits of lima beans and potatoes. He was most famished.

"You can assure your ma I'll be on my way right after sunset," he replied to the message I bore from her. "Tell her I don't want folks to see me in town . . . by daylight."

I nodded, looking at his empty plate.

"Your ma has taken awful good care of you, Les. I observed that right away. I'm grateful to her for that, you can tell her. The day I get back on my feet, son, I will see to it that a lot of the things owin' to you will be yours. . . . Count on me."

I didn't quite know what he meant then, but I was pleased he felt I deserved something. Ma didn't often make me feel deserving.

Short Papa got up from the table, loosened his suspenders under his suit coat, felt in his breast pocket as he kept clearing his throat, and then sat down again as he said, "Matter of fact, Les, I have brought you a little something. But first you best take this plate back to the kitchen, for you know how fussy your ma is about dirty dishes standing around."

I rushed with the plate back to the kitchen and on the double back to Short Papa, and sat down beside him on a little taboret which we use for sitting on.

"I want you to promise me, though, you won't lose it after I give it to you," Short Papa said solemnly.

I promised.

"Cross your heart and all that." Short Papa sort of grinned, but I knew he was dead serious and wanted me to be.

"Cross my heart, Papa."

"All right, Lester. Then here it is."

He handed me a great, really heavy gold watch with a massive chain a-hanging from it.

"Don't you worry now, Les. It is not stolen. It is your great-grandpa's watch. All during my most recent trouble I kept it in a safety deposit vault over at Moortown. I got behind on the annual rent payments when I was in jail, but the bank trusted me, Les, and they kept it. I have paid up for the arrears and this watch is yours. It has been in the family for well over a hundred years, you can count on that."

I was not really glad to get the watch, and yet I wanted it too. I wanted also to show Short Papa I was grateful, and so I hugged and kissed him. His eyes watered a little and he turned away from me, and then he laughed and slapped my shoulder several times.

"Keep it in a safe place, Les, for beyond what it's worth, which ain't inconsiderable, it's your old pa and his pa, and his pa before him, that owned it. Understand? Course you do . . ."

After Short Papa left, I sat for a long time on the back porch listening to my watch tick. It had a powerful beat to it. From behind me I could hear Ma talking with Sister Ruth about the dress they were making for her wedding. Ruth was going to be married in June.

I considered how Short Papa's sudden arrival and departure had made no impression on them. He might as well have been the man who comes to collect the old papers and tin cans. Yet he was Ruth's father too.

"You take my word for it, Les, things are going to be hunky-dory one day for all of us again."

That was what Pa had said to me as he slipped out the back way in the gathering darkness, and like the ticking of my watch those words kept pounding in my ears.

Ma had made me ashamed of Papa always reminding me of the many times he had been sent to jail for a short stretch (hence his nickname), and once out, he would only be sent back again, and so on and so forth, but there was now something about the way this watch ticking away in my possession made me feel not only different about Papa and his pa and his pa before him, I felt for the first time I was connected with somebody, or with something. I felt I had a basic, you see. But I didn't want anybody to know I had the watch, and I also felt that I would never see Short Papa again, that he had come back to speak his piece and be gone for good.

As a result I felt awful crushed that Short Papa had been entertained so miserly by Ma, being fed on the back porch like a tramp, and then dismissed. But then Ma's attitude toward Pa was hard to fathom, for though she never wanted any more to do with him she never said anything about getting a divorce. She just didn't want any more men around, for one thing, and then, as she said, why go to the bother of divorcing somebody when you was already divorced from him for good and all. . . .

I kept the watch under my pillow at night, and I wound it cautiously and slow twice a day, like he had instructed me, and I never let it out of my sight whilst I was awake, keeping it with me at all times. I could not imagine being without it ever now.

After a couple to three months of this great care with his watch, and to tell the truth getting a little weary sometimes with the worry and guardianship bestowed on it, the polishing and keeping it when unused in its own little cotton case, and also seeing it was hid from Ma, for I feared she might claim it away from me for what Pa owed her, I remember the time it happened: It was an unsteady spring afternoon, when it couldn't make up its mind whether it was still winter or shirt-sleeves weather, and I had gone to the Regal Pool Parlors to watch the fellows shoot pool, for at this time their hard-fast rule there was that nobody under sixteen was allowed to play, but you could be a spectator provided you kept your mouth shut.

Absorbed in the games and the talk of the older fellows, before I was aware of it all the shadows had lengthened outside and the first streetlights had begun to pop on, and so then almost automatically I began to lift the chain to my watch, and as I did so I was all at once reminded of another time further back when Short Papa had been teaching me to fish and he had said nervously, "Pull up your rod, Les, you've got a bite there!" And I had pulled of course and felt the rod heavy at first and weighted but then pulling harder I got this terrible lightness, and yanking the pole to shore there was nothing on the hook at all, including no bait neither. And pulling now on the watch chain I drew up nothing from my pocket. My watch was gone. I got faint-sick all over. I was too shaky in fact to get up and start looking. I was pretty sure, nonplussed though I was, that I had not lost it here in the Regal Pool Parlors, but I went over to Bud Hughes the manager, who knew me and my family, and told him.

Bud studied my face a long time, and then finally I saw he believed me, but he kept asking a few more questions, like where I had got the watch in the first place, and when. I lied to him then, because if he had knowed it come direct from Short Papa he would have thought it was stolen. So I told him the far side of the truth, that it was from my great-grandfather, passed on to me, and this seemed to satisfy him, and he said he would be on the lookout.

Almost every day thereafter on the way home from school I stopped in at the Regal to see if they had any news about my watch, and it got to be a kind of joke there with the customers and with Bud especially. I think they were almost half-glad to see me show up so regular, and inquire.

"No news, though, yet about your great-grandfather's watch," Bud Hughes would generally manage to quip at some time during my visit, and he would wink at me.

Then the joke about the missing watch having run its course, no mention was finally ever made of it again, and then after a while I quit going to the Regal entirely.

I held on to the chain, though, like for dear life, and never left it out of my grasp if I could help it.

During this period of what must have been a year or two, Ma would often study me more carefully than usual, as if she had decided there was something wrong somewhere, but then finally decided she didn't want to know maybe what it was, for she had enough other worries nagging away at her.

About this time, school being out, and the long summer vacation getting under way, I got me a job in a concession at Auglaize Amusement Park selling Cracker Jack and candy bars in the arcade that faces the river. They give me a nice white uniform and cap, and for the first time the girls began making eyes at me. . . . I realized that summer I was growing up, and I also realized I would soon be able to leave Ma for good and fend for myself.

On the way to work I would pass this fortune-teller's booth early each P.M. and the lady who told the fortunes was usually seated in a silk upholstered armchair outside, and got to know me by sight. She wasn't exactly young or old, and went under the name Madame Amelia. She was also very pleasant to me partly because she knowed I worked in the concession. One time right out of the blue she told me she would be happy to give a nice young boy starting out a free reading but not to wait too long to come in and take advantage of it, now business was still a bit slack.

I had sort of a crush on a young girl who come in now with her soldier boyfriend and bought popcorn from me, and I wanted like everything to find out her name and if she was going to be married to her boyfriend. So I decided finally to take advantage of Madame Amelia's invitation and offer. . . . The fortune-telling booth with the smell of incense and jingle of little wind chimes and the perfume of red jasmine which she wore on her own person, the thought of the girl I loved and her soldier friend sort of went right out of my head and vanished into thin air.

I felt an old hurt begin to throb inside me.

Madame Amelia at first sort of flailed around asking me a few leading questions, such as where I had grown up, if I was the only boy in the family and if I had worked in the concession before, and so on—all just to get her warmed up, as I later found out was the practice with "readers." But then just before she began the actual fortune in earnest, she held her breast, her eyes closed tight, and she looked so tortured and distressed I thought she was about to have a heart attack, but it was all part also of her getting in touch with the "hidden forces" which was to direct her sorting out your fortune.

Then she got very calm and quiet, and looked me straight in the eye.

I stirred under her searching scowl.

"Before I begin, Lester," she said, shading her brow, "I must ask you something, for you are a good subject, my dear—I can tell —and unusually receptive for a young boy. What I would get for you, therefore, would come from deeper down than just any ordinary fortune. Is that clear?"

She looked at me very narrowly. "In other words, Lester, do you want to hear the truth or do you just want the usual amusement park rigmarole?"

"The truth, Madame Amelia," I said as resolutely as I could.

She nodded, and touched my hand.

"You have had two losses, Lester," she began now at once in a booming voice. "But you know only about one of them, I see."

The words *the truth* seemed to form again and again on my tongue like the first wave of severe nausea.

"As I say," she was going on, "you have lost two things precious to you. A gift, and a man who loves you very deeply.

"The hand that gave you the gift which you have not been able to locate, that hand has been cold a long time, and will soon turn to dust. You will never see him again in this life."

I gave out a short cry, but Madame Amelia pointed an outstretched finger at me which would have silenced a whole auditorium.

"Long since turned to dust," she went on pitilessly. "But the gift which he bestowed on you is not lost." Her voice was now soft and less scary. "I see a bed, Lester, on which you sleep. . . . The gift so precious to both the giver and the receiver you will find within the mattress . . . in a small opening."

I do not even remember leaving Madame Amelia's, or recall working the rest of the afternoon in the popcorn concession. . . . I do know I ran most of the way home.

Mama was giving a big party for her bridge club, and for once she was in a good humor, so she said very little to me as I rushed past upstairs to my bedroom.

Mama always made my bed so good, I hated to take off the hand-sewn coverlet and the immaculate just-changed and ironed sheet, but I had to know if Madame Amelia was telling me the truth. . . . I hoped and prayed she was wrong, that she had lied, and that I would not find the watch, for if that part of the fortune was not true, neither would be the other part about the hand of the bestower.

I searched and searched but could find no little aperture where my watch would have slipped down in the mattress, until when about to give up, all at once I see under one of the buttonlike doohickeys a sort of small opening. . . . My hand delved down, my heart came into my mouth, I felt the cold metal, I pulled it out, it was my gold watch.

But instead of the joy at having it back, I felt as bad as if I had killed somebody. Sitting there with the timepiece which I now wound carefully, I lost all track of my surroundings. I sat there on the unmade bed for I don't know how long, hardly looking at my long-lost friend, which ticked on and on uncomfortingly.

"Lester?" I heard Mama's troubled voice. "Why, where on earth did you ever get that beautiful watch?"

I looked up at her, and then I told it all to her. . . .

She looked at the tousled condition of sheets, coverlet, and mattress, but there come from her no criticism or scolding.

She held the watch now in her own palm and gazed at it carefully but sort of absentmindedly.

"You should have told me, Lester, and not kept it locked in your own heart all this time. You should confide in Mama more. Just look at you, too, you're growing into a handsome young man right in front of my eyes."

A queer kind of sob escaped from her. . . .

"Where is Short Papa, do you suppose?" I got out at last as she took my hand.

Mama smoothed her hair briefly, then she went on: "I have wondered and wondered how I was to tell you all these months, Lester, and I see that as usual I must have did the wrong thing where you and Short Papa are concerned. But you realize I learned of his death weeks after the event. . . . And then weeks and weeks after that I heard he had been buried in accord with his firm instructions that there was to be no funeral and nobody was to be notified back here of his passing. . . ."

I nodded, meaning I did not blame her, but kept looking hard at the watch, and thinking there could be no place safe enough now for it, and that it must never part from me again.

"I've always wanted to do what was best, Lester," Mama went on, "but parents too are only after all flesh and blood as someday you will find out for yourself."

She dried her eyes on her tea apron and then touched me softly on the cheek and started to make up the bed, and at the very last to make a final touch she got out her old-fashioned bedspread from the cedar chest and put that over the rayon coverlet.

Mud Toe the Cannibal

A songster by the name of Baby Bundy was accustomed to thrill his church and congregation every Sunday and Thursday in New York by singing anthems, solos, and old hymn tunes. Once in the midst of a long cadenza a dragon fly stole into his mouth and was almost swallowed. Instead of giving forth his next note Baby Bundy exhaled to the congregation's wonder the golden fly, who came sailing straight ahead to freedom.

The dragon fly lived near the lily pond and had for companions midges, golden fish, frogs with blazing green on their coats, and a youthful cannibal named Mud Toe. The cannibal was very doleful because he knew no other cannibals and furthermore it was against the law at the lily pond to eat anything but vegetables. Sometimes the very thought of another vegetable made him scream so loudly the golden fish, the butterflies, and frogs all fled in fear and trembling. The dragon fly, however, who had, after all, been swallowed in church by the songster, was not afraid, for he knew, even if the cannibal swallowed him, he'd soon give him up again. Nobody can enjoy a dragon fly in his stomach.

The dragon fly said, one day, "Cannibal, what is the matter with you, that you mope and scowl and droop?"

"The matter, Dragon Fly, is I know only fish and turtles, and I have to eat sea kale," he complained, "when it's people I long for."

"But you've been living here with us in the lily pond for years now without eating anybody, and look at you: strong, bronzed, with an erect spine and clear eyes! What more do you want out of life, Mud Toe?" (Mud Toe was his adopted name.)

"On the other hand," the dragon fly went on, "Baby Bundy, who lives on the other side of the shore, has to sing for a living in New York (where he swallowed me by mistake), and rides in overage subway cars with people unwashed as midnight and cross as starving tigers. Yet he goes his way summer, fall, and winter, and doesn't give up."

"Then I will visit Baby Bundy and see how he keeps his sweet disposition," the cannibal announced.

Mud Toe went on foot to Greenwich Village, where Bundy lived. His appearance did not startle anybody too much except perhaps a traffic policeman. Yet all Mud Toe had on was a shark's tooth or two, sensibly arranged over his torso.

When the cannibal got to Bank Street, he stopped a boy with scowling blue eyes whom later he was to find to be a thespian.

"Do you know the way to Baby Bundy, the songster?" Mud Toe inquired.

"I do, but why should I tell you?" the thespian scolded. "And, besides, why don't you wash your hair? It's full of water lilies."

"I am a retired cannibal," Mud Toe explained (ignoring the personal remark), "not through age, but by law and regulation. I want to visit Baby Bundy to see how he keeps cheerful in the summer, when I am depressed summer, spring, winter, and fall."

"I have just come from Baby Bundy, matter of fact," the thespian volunteered. "And I think he would enjoy at least playing the piano for such as you. He never tires doing so, as far as I can see. . . ."

"Thank you for the suggestion, Thespian," Mud Toe replied, "but you still haven't told me how to reach the songster."

"Go—" the thespian commenced with his mouth tightly closed and his eyes blazing, "go to the big building that overlooks Suicide Docks, and before you get too close to the water, turn around three times and whistle. The wind will tell you which way to turn at that time."

Mud Toe thanked the thespian and went on his way.

Night was falling when he reached Suicide Docks, and there was no wind. The cannibal sat down on the curb and began to cry. The people about him were so dirty and cross he had no desire to eat any of them. There was no air, the trucks gave out black curls of smoke, and several children were beating an old woman because she refused to buy them frozen fudge bars.

Mud Toe became very homesick for his pond, the dragon fly, and the turtle (whom he had almost married during the cold winter of two years ago).

Just then he heard a piano, coming from above.

"Is that you, Bundy?" Mud Toe cried from the curb.

A window went up on story two, and a brown-eyed young man eating two pieces of chocolate cake yelled down, "Who's taking my name in vain again?"

"It's Mud Toe," came the reply. "A cannibal forbidden to practice his calling. May I come up and see how you keep cheerful in the Good Old Summertime?"

"*Mud Toe!*" Bundy mused over the name. "Why, haven't I seen you mentioned in *Remarkable People You May Have Missed,* the celebrity calendar?"

"No way!" Mud Toe replied in the lingo he had heard near Suicide Docks. "I have lived practically all my life with the dragon fly and the turtle, and a few golden fish at the lily pond."

"Very well!" Baby Bundy consented. "If you don't mind only a brief visit, well and good, for I'm due uptown in half an hour at the studio of the Slavic Queen for an accompanist session, so come up and I'll tell you how I keep happy and cool in the summer."

"I declare! You don't care much for clothes, do you?" Baby B. exclaimed when Mud Toe entered his big studio with the forty-foot ceilings and the five-acre rehearsal rooms. "I guess, though, your physique can stand airing." The songster went on looking at his visitor with careful scrutiny.

"What can I fix you to drink?" Bundy inquired as the cannibal continued on his part to gaze open-mouthed about him. "I have coconut glacé, sarsaparilla shake, and Hershey dream soda."

"I'll take the whole shebang, Baby B., and while I'm drinking I'd like you to play me one of your 'Happy Hour Melodies' people are always talking about."

"I will make you a Hershey dream soda, as it's all mixed and ready," Baby B. proposed, and almost instantly proffered the cannibal a king-size cup of frothy imported cocoa.

"Mmm," Mud Toe panted, "we don't get this at the pond, I can tell you."

"Doesn't surprise me, for prices have never been higher, Mud Toe, yet somehow I go on eating and sleeping in the big town."

"You have lots of room, here, don't you?" Mud Toe went on with his observations of the studio.

"Only enough though for myself," Baby B. said nervously. "I've had my share of roomers and sleeping companions. They just don't pan out for an artist. I have a lot on my mind, and I don't need steady company. It's worse than *lonely!*"

"Well, as it's not getting any earlier out, shall we begin?" Baby

Bundy proposed when Mud Toe made no rejoinder to his observations about living by himself. "Gather round the piano, why don't you, and I'll play a Happy Melody."

Seating himself before his grand piano, the songster closed his eyes tightly for a moment, then plunged both hands into resounding, cheerful, ear-splitting chords.

"Oh, oh, oh, and oh!" cried the cannibal.

"What's amiss now?" the songster wondered, leaving off playing.

"I'm only exclaiming with joy," Mud Toe retorted. "Please continue the concert."

The songster then played a number of his famous Happy Songs, one after the other in rapid fire.

What was the piano player's astonishment, though, when he saw the cannibal looking down on him from atop the forty-foot ceiling.

"What on earth, or rather how in heaven's name did you get up there!" Baby B. vociferated.

"I rose automatically," the cannibal tried to explain. "Your songs are wings and have made me fly! I can never thank you enough!"

Baby B. now played a melancholy albeit still sweet melody, and the cannibal slowly descended.

Kneeling at the feet of the songster, Mud Toe cried, "How can I ever repay you for such happiness?"

As he spoke he kissed the pianist's feet hungrily.

"Now, now," the songster admonished uneasily. "No need for excessive demonstrations, you know."

Rising and bowing, the young cannibal said, "May I ask you a favor?" But even as he was making his request, Mud Toe's eyes caught sight of a ticking clock.

"Is that timepiece fast?" the visitor wondered. "Because it doesn't jibe with my dragon fly–turtle sun chart!"

"That clock is about twenty minutes fast, Mud Toe," Baby B. admitted. "I'm a 'latey,' you know, and so have to hurry all day because I have this natural inclination to come late."

"To make a long matter short, Baby B.," Mud Toe began after a great deal of bashfulness and hesitation, "you have made me feel entirely different about life. You have also cheered me up tremendously. I guess I can bear my lot now."

Baby B. lowered his eyes in embarrassed pleasure.

"To go back to the favor I mentioned. Will you permit me to kiss you good and hard as a farewell gesture?" the cannibal inquired. "Please," he said as he saw his host hesitate. "Don't start so. I gave up eating people long ago, though I am still a young man by the lily pond calendar. Only fourteen. Would you mind shaving off your moustache though, before I kiss you, Baby B.?"

"Why, I certainly would, Mud Toe!" The songster spoke with indignation. "My moustache is part of my stock-in-trade. I'm really quite annoyed you could ask such a favor."

"Don't be annoyed with me," Mud Toe implored. "I'll kiss you right through the hair."

"Well, get along with it, then, why don't you, because I'm due uptown in just a few more minutes."

Baby B. closed his eyes, and Mud Toe bent down and kissed him once gently, then again and again, each time with more force.

"I believe that is enough." Baby B. opened his eyes smartly and looked questioningly at Mud Toe.

"Just one more kiss for the road," Mud Toe coaxed.

"All right, but then stop."

"Thank you, Baby B.," Mud Toe responded, wiping his mouth dry and then kissing him again.

"Ah," the cannibal said. "The dragon fly was right. . . . You have made me feel I can go on living at the lily pond. . . . I think I've changed disposition mostly owing to the Hershey soda, maybe. No, it was your songs, of course! No, it was your forty-foot ceiling! No, it was your kisses! No, it was—"

"I'm sorry!" Baby Bundy interrupted, and ushered the cannibal to the door. "But you'll have to go now. I have to vocalize a bit and spray my tonsils prior to my task as accompanist to the Slavic Queen. . . . But thank you so much for coming, Mud Toe, and thank you also for your compliments! We all need *them.*"

"Just one more kiss, Baby B., at the threshold," Mud Toe implored.

"Oh, stop it!" the songster pretended to scold while allowing Mud Toe to take another kiss. "Now go back to your pond!"

And Baby B. closed the door.

The songster stood on the threshold for several minutes, thinking about his visitor.

It had been an unusual afternoon, no question about it, and to tell the truth nobody kisses quite so tenderly as a retired cannibal.

How I Became a Shadow

How I Became a Shadow, how I live in the defile of mountains, and how I lost my Cock.

By Pablo Rangel.

Gonzago is to blame. He said, "That rooster is too good for a pet. He belongs in the cockfight. You give him to me, you owe me favors. I am your cousin. Give him up."

"Never, Gonzago," I replied. *"Nunca.* I raised the little fellow from almost an egg. I never render him to you, *primo."*

"Shut your mouth that flies are always crawling in. Shut up, you whelp, when I command. That cock is too good for a pet. Hear me. You will give him up, and we will both make money. You belly-ache, you say you are always broke, and then when the chance comes to make something you tell your cousin to go hang his ass up to dry. No, Pablo, listen good. The cock is as good as mine because of all the favors I done you, remember. Hear me. I am going to come take him and will fetch you another cock to take his place. Then I will enter your cock at the fight and we will get rich."

"I will not render him," I told Gonzago. "I will keep my pet by me forever. You are not man enough anyhow to take him from me. If Jesus Himself come down from the clouds and said, 'Pablo, I require you to render me your cock as an offering,' I would reply, 'Jesus, go back and hang again on the cross, I will not render my pet, die, Jesus, this time forever.' "

"Ha, Jesus, always Him," Gonzago snorted. "As if He cared about your cock or whether he fights or don't fight. You fool, even your shit isn't brown. You were born to lose. But I will teach you yet. You will not order your cousin about just because you have no wits and need others to watch out for you. . . . Hear me. . . . Tonight I will come for the cock. Hear? Tonight, for tomorrow is the cockfight, and we will win, Pablo. I have been teaching your Placido to fight while you were waiting table at the big American hotel. *Caray,* you did not even notice? See, Placido is ready."

"Ah, so that is why he is so thin and don't eat, evil Gonzago. . . . Never, never say you will take him, though. . . . Look into my eyes, cousin, what do you see there, look good."

"I see nothing in your eyes but stubborn pigheaded pride. Starve to death, why don't you, see if I care. Go with your ass to the wind forever, or die and be dead forever like Jesus. . . . But I will take your cock when I want to on account of you owe me your life, you owe me money for your keep since a boy, you *owe owe owe!*"

"Nothing, Gonzago. I owe you nothing, and won't never give up what I don't owe for. Kill me if you want to. . . . Here is my machete my grandfather passed on to me. Take it and cut me in two, see if I care!"

~·~·~·~·~

That night, Gonzago returned with a big burlap sack with an iron piece that shut over the mouth. He took Placido from his little warm box. My pet gave out piteous little cries as he was grasped. I rushed over to him, but Gonzago had put him already in the sack, and run like the wind and got in his truck and drove off to the cock ring.

I followed on foot. I did not know what I did. I smoked something, smoked it many times. I lost track of time smoking it. Then there I was at the fight sitting in the front row of seats, watching through blue clouds of smoke, not knowing yet one rooster from another.

Then I saw the light of my life come forward, the pet I all alone had raised and whose name I called: "Placido! Placido! *Amor mío!*" I yelled and shouted until the police came and took me outside and clubbed me for kicking them. I fell down on the curb and talked to its cold stones.

After the air revived me, I stole back into the arena. Gonzago stood in the center of a knot of men. "You can have your pet back now." He spoke to me inhaling on a cigar with an end like a volcano. "Over there, *primo*"—he pointed—"behind the piled-up folding chairs and the flag."

I went there and looked down on the ground where he had pointed.

At first I see nothing, just earth and a few cigar wrappers. Then I made out his form at last. He was all wings spread on the black soil, but with no eyes. Placido had no eyes! But I knew him still by his gold and red feathers, and his pretty head. But no eyes!

I waited until I got possession of myself, and my heart had quit thundering in my ears. Then I came back to Gonzago. I smiled. Gonzago relaxed. "I invite you to a drink, Pablo."

"Fine," I agreed.

We went to the saloon. Gonzago ordered the best tequila. He paid, he ordered again, the money showered from his hands covered with rings.

When he was feeling his liquor, I pretended friendship and patted him. "Gonzago," I said, "you are a very clever man, and have my good at heart."

"*Gracias, primo,*" he said, and he relaxed some more.

"Because of that," I went on, "I want to share again with you. I have another cock you do not know about. A great scrapper and bigger than Placido."

"Is that so?" Gonzago wondered.

"Yes, *primo,* come closer, please, and I will show him to you. This one is a winner. Here, here, look, Gonzago," and I uncovered the little machete I had hidden under my coat.

I cut swiftly like a parcel of winds across Gonzago's unprotected brow. I reddened his eyes with one blow of my machete after another. I cut his eyes to holes like those that were left in Placido's head.

"Placido, *amor,* rest happy, Placido, be avenged. Die, Gonzago, with blind *ojos,* die, blind eyes!"

Then I ran to the mountains where I move like hawks or a mountain cat, or vesper winds. But I keep Placido's feathers against my heart. I live in the defile of mountains. I am called Shadow.

Dawn

It wasn't as if Timmy had made his living posing nude and having his picture in the flesh magazines. Tim modeled clothes mostly and was making good money. But he did do one underwear modeling job and that was the one his dad saw in North Carolina. Wouldn't you know it would be! So his dad thought there must be more and worse ones. Nude ones, you know. His dad was a pill.

His dad came in to New York from this place he had lived in all his life. Population about four hundred people, probably counting the dead.

Well, his dad was something. He arrived in the dead of night or rather when the first streaks of morning were reaching the Empire State.

"Where is Timmy?" he said without even saying hello or telling me who he was. (I recognized him from one of Tim's snapshots.) He pushed right past me into the front room like a house detective with the passkey.

"Well, where is he?" He roared his question this time.

"Mr. Jaqua," I replied. "He just stepped out for a moment."

"I bet," the old man quipped. "Where does he sleep when he is to home?" he went on while looking around the apartment as if for clues.

I showed him the little room down the hall. He took a quick look inside and clicked his tongue in disapproval, and rushed right on back to the front room and helped himself to the big easy chair.

He brought out a raggedy clipping from his breast pocket.

"Have you laid eyes on this?" He beckoned for me to come over and see what he was holding.

It was the magazine ad of Tim all right, posing in very scanty red shorts.

I colored by way of reply and Mr. Jaqua studied me.

"I suppose there are more of these in other places," he accused me.

"Well!" He raised his voice when I did not reply.

"I don't poke my nose into his business," I said lamely. I colored again.

"I can't blame you if you don't." He was a bit conciliatory.

"See here, Freddy. . . . You are Freddy, I suppose, unless he's changed roommates. Pay me mind. I wanted Tim to be a lawyer and make good money and settle down, but he was stagestruck from a boy of ten." Mr. Jaqua seemed to be talking to a large assembly of people, and he looked out through my small apartment window into the street. "I've sent him enough money to educate four boys," he went on. "I could even have stood it, I think, if he had made good on the stage. But where are the parts he should have found? You tell me!" His eyes moved away from outdoors, and his gaze rested on me.

"He failed," the old man finished and looked at the underwear ad fiercely.

"But Tim had some good parts, Mr. Jaqua. Even on Broadway." I began my defense, but I was so stricken by this man's rudeness and insensitivity that I found myself finally just studying him as a spectacle.

"There's a screw loose somewhere." He ignored my bits of information about Tim's acting career. "I've come to take him home, Freddy."

He looked at me now very sadly as if by studying me, the underwear ad, the acting career, and the loose screw would all at last be explained.

"See here. Everybody saw this ad back home." He tapped the clipping with his finger. "The damned thing was in the barbershop, then it turned up in the pool parlor, I'm told, and the dentist's office, and God knows maybe finally in Sunday school and church."

"It paid good money, though, Mr. Jaqua."

"Good money," he repeated and I remembered then he was a trial lawyer.

"I should think it would, Freddy," he sneered as if finally dismissing me as a witness.

"It's very tough being an actor, Mr. Jaqua." I interrupted his silence. "I know because I am one. There's almost no serious theater today, you see."

"Do you have any coffee in the house, Freddy?" he said after another prolonged silence.

"I have fresh breakfast coffee, sir. Would you like a cup?"

"Yes, that would be nice." He folded the advertisement of the red shorts and put it back in his pocket until it would be produced again later on.

"What I'd like better, though," he said after sipping a little of my strong brew, "would you let me lie down on his bed and get some rest pending his arrival?"

Mr. Jaqua never waited for my nod of approval, for he went immediately to the bedroom and closed the door energetically.

~~~~~

"Your dad is here," I told Timmy as he came through the door.

"No," he moaned. He turned deathly pale, almost green. "Jesus," he whimpered.

"He's lying down on your bed," I explained.

"Oh, Freddy," he said. "I was afraid this would happen one day. . . . What does he want?"

"Seems he saw you in that underwear ad."

Tim made a grimace with his lips that looked like the smile on a man I once saw lying dead of gunshot wounds on the street. I looked away.

"He expects you to go home with him, Timmy," I warned him.

"Oh, Christ in heaven!" He sat down in the big chair, and picked up the coffee cup his dad had left and sipped some of it. It was my turn to show a queer smile.

Tim just sat on there then for an hour or more while I pretended to do some cleaning up of our apartment, all the while watching him every so often and being scared at what I saw.

Then all at once, as if he had heard his cue, he stood up, squared his shoulders, muttered something, and without a look or word to me, he went to the bedroom door, opened it, and went in.

At first the voices were low, almost whispers, then they rose in a high, dizzy crescendo, and there was cursing and banging and so on as in all domestic quarrels. Then came a silence, and after that silence I could hear Tim weeping hard. I had never heard him or seen him cry in all our three years of living together. I felt terribly disappointed somehow. He was crying like a little boy.

I sat down stunned as if my own father had come back from

the dead and pointed out all my shortcomings and my poor record as an actor and a man.

Finally they came out together, and Tim had his two big suitcases in hand.

"I'm going home for a while, Freddy," he told me, and this time he smiled his old familiar smile. "Take this." He extended a big handful of bills.

"I don't want it, Timmy."

His father took the bills from him then—there were several hundred-dollar ones—and pressed them hard into my hand. Somehow I could accept them from Mr. Jaqua.

"Tim will write you when he gets settled back home. Won't you, Tim?" the old man inquired as they went out the door.

After their footsteps died away, I broke down and cried, not like a young boy, but like a baby. I cried for over an hour. And strange to say I felt almost refreshed at shedding so many bitter tears. I realized how badly I had suffered in New York, and how much I loved Timmy, though I knew he did not love me very much in return. And I knew then as I do now I would never see him again.

The Candles
of Your Eyes

As late as two years ago a powerfully built black man used to walk up and down East Fourth Street carrying a placard in purple and crocus letters which read:

> I AM A MURDERER
> Why Don't They Give Me the Chair?
> Signed, Soldier

Strangers to the East Village would inquire who Soldier was and who it was he had murdered.

There were always some of us from Louisiana who had time enough to tell the inquirer Soldier's story, which evolved as much around Beaut Orleans as it did the placard-carrier.

Beauty Orleans, or Beaut, who came from the same section of Louisiana as Soldier, grew more handsome the older he got, we thought, but he was always from the time he appeared in the

Village a cynosure for all eyes. At seventeen Beaut looked some-times only thirteen. His most unusual feature, though, happened to be his eyes, which someone said reminded one of flashes of heat lightning.

How Beauty lived before Soldier took him over nobody ever tried to figure out. He had no education, no training, no skills. He wore the same clothes winter and summer, and was often even on frigid December days barefoot. In summer he put on a Ger-man undershirt which he pulled down almost as far as his knees. He found most of his clothes outside the back door of a repertory theater.

After considerable coaxing and begging Beauty agreed to settle down with Soldier in a run-down half-vacant building, not far from the Bowery.

Because of Beaut's extraordinary good looks and his strange eyes, artists were always clamoring to make drawings of him.

His friend Soldier, whose own eyes were the color of slightly new pennies, protected or perhaps imprisoned Beaut out of his love for the boy. If you wanted to get permission to draw Beaut, you had to go straight to Soldier first and finagle the arrange-ments.

Soldier would hesitate a long while with a suing artist, would leaf through an old ledger he had found in the same theater Beaut got his clothes from, and finally, after arguing and scolding, would arrive at a just price, and Beaut was begrudgingly allowed to leave for a calculated number of hours.

I don't know which of the two loved the other the most, Beaut Soldier or Soldier Beaut.

Soldier used to hold Beaut in his arms and lullaby him in a big rocking chair which they had found in good shape left behind on the street by looters.

He rocked Beaut in the chair as one would a doll. It was their

chief occupation, their sole entertainment. It was an unforgetta-
ble sight, midnight-black strapping Soldier holding the somewhat
delicate, though really tough, Beaut. If you looked in on them in
the dark, you seemed to see only Beaut asleep in what looked like
the dark branches of a tree.

Soldier earned for them both, either by begging or stealing. But
he was not considered a professional thief even by the police. Just
light-fingered when the need was pressing.

Soldier insisted Beaut always wear a gold chain he had picked
up from somewhere, but the younger man did not like the feel
of metal against his throat. He said it reminded him of a gun
pointed at him. But in the end he gave in and wore the chain.

People in the Village wondered how these two could go on so
long together. But it was finally understood that Beaut and Soldier
had reached some kind of perfection in their love for one another.
They had no future, and no past—just the *now* in which Soldier
rocked Beauty on his knees and kissed his smooth satiny reddish-
gold hair.

"Beaut," Soldier said once near the end of their time together,
gazing at him out of his brown-penny eyes, "you are my morning,
noon, and night. But especially noon, you hear? Broad noon.
Why, if the sun went out, and no stars shined, and I had you,
Beaut, I wouldn't give a snap if all them luminaries was snuffed
out. You'd shine to make me think they was still out there bla-
zin'."

Then he would rock Beaut and lullaby him as the night settled
down over the city.

We knew it couldn't last. Nothing perfect and beautiful has
any future. And these two were already overdue in their paradise
together. Doom is what perfect love is always headed for.

So then one night Soldier did not come back to that shell of
a building they had lived together in.

Beaut stirred after a while in the chair, like a child in his mother's body wanting to be born. Still, no Soldier.

Hunger at last drove Beaut out into the street. Outside, he rubbed his eyes and stared about as if he had been asleep for many considerable years.

"Where's Soldier?" he asked of everybody he met, friend or total stranger.

By way of reply, we gave him food and drink. No one thought to rock him.

As days and weeks passed, the young boy got older-looking, but if anything more beautiful. His eyes located deep in his skull looked like little birthday candles flickering. A few wrinkles began forming around those candlelike eyes. Some of his teeth came out, but he looked handsome still even without them.

All he ever said when he said anything was "Where is Soldier at?"

Beaut stole some reading glasses from a secondhand store in order to go over the ledger which Soldier had left behind and into which his black friend was accustomed to put down sentences when he was not rocking Beaut.

But the sentences in the ledger, it appeared, all said the same thing over and again, often in the same wording, like the copybook of a schoolboy who is learning to spell.

The sentences read: "Soldier loves Beaut. He's my sky and land and deep blue sea. Beaut, don't ever leave me. Beaut, never stop loving me and letting me love you. You hear me?"

Beaut rocked in the chair, singing his own lullaby to himself. He broke his glasses, but managed to read the ledger anyhow, for in any case he had got by heart the few repeated sentences Soldier had put down in it.

"He'll come back," Beaut told Orley Austin, a Negro ex-boxer from Mississippi. "I know Soldier."

One day Orley came into the room with the rocking chair, and closed the door loudly behind him. He looked at Beaut. He spat on his palms and rubbed them together vigorously.

"Say," Beaut raised his voice. Orley bent down and kissed Beaut on the crown of his head, and put his right hand over Beaut's heart, thus testifying he had come to take Soldier's place in the rocking-chair room.

So they began where Soldier had left off, the new lover and Beaut together, but though the younger man was not so lonesome with Orley around, you could see he was not quite as satisfied with the ex-boxer as he had been with Soldier—despite the fact that if anything Orley rocked Beaut more than Soldier had. He could rock him all night long because he smoked too much stuff.

Then you remember that terrible winter that broke all weather records. Usually New York doesn't have such fierce cold as say Boston or northern Maine, though for those from Louisiana even a little taste of Northern winter is too much. And you have got to remember the house with the rocking-chair room didn't have much in the way of a furnace. The pipes all froze, the front windows turned to a kind of iceberg, and even the rats were found ice-stiff on the stairs.

Ice hung from the big high ceiling like it had grown chandeliers.

The staircase collapsed from broken pipes and accumulations of giant icicles.

At the first break in the weather, wouldn't you know, Soldier returned. He had some difficulty getting to the upstairs on account of there was no stairs now, only piles of lumber, but he crawled and crept his way up to the rocking-chair room.

What he saw froze him like the ice had frozen the house.

He saw his place taken by Orley, who was holding Beaut in his arms in the chair, their lips pressed tightly together, their hands holding one another more securely than Soldier had ever dared hold Beaut. They looked to him like flowers under deep mountain streams, but motionless like the moon in November.

"Explain me" was all Soldier was able to get out from his lips. "Explain me!"

When they did not answer, and did not so much as open their eyes, he brought out his stolen gun.

"Tell me what I am lookin' at ain't so," he thought he said to them.

When nobody spoke, he cocked his gun.

He waited another minute in the silence, then he fired all the bullets. But as they flew through the melting air, he saw something was wrong even with the bullets, for though they hit their target, their target deflected them like stone, not flesh and blood.

We have decided that Soldier had gone crazy even before he emptied the gun on the two lovers, but the realization his bullets did not reach flesh and blood caused him to lose his mind completely.

After the shooting he went to the police station and charged himself. The police hardly said two words to him, and took down nothing he said. But they did finally get around to going to the rocking-chair room in their own good time. They must have seen at once that Beaut and Orley had been dead for days, maybe weeks, long before Soldier reached them. No gun can kill people who have frozen to death.

Every day for many weeks Soldier went to the police precinct and confessed to murder. Some of the cops even pretended to take down what he said. They gave him cigarettes and bottled soda.

Soldier lives in a different building now with an older white boy. But every day, especially on Sundays, he carries up and down Fourth Street this placard, whose letters are beginning to fade:

I AM A MURDERER
Why Don't They Give Me the Chair?

Rapture

"I wouldn't have known you!" Mrs. Muir spoke to her brother. "You've grown so tall, and you're so deeply tanned. Oh, Kent, it's really you, then?"

Kent put down his two valises, and kissed her dryly on the cheek.

"You haven't changed much, though, Gladys. The same sweet smile, and sky-blue eyes." He hugged her ever so gently then.

Kent was Gladys Muir's half-brother. He had an extended furlough from the army, where he was stationed in West Germany. Before his assignment there he had been in the Middle East, and before that somewhere in the Pacific. But now, though still a young man, he was a few years over thirty, he was free from his military service at least for a while.

He had been given so long a furlough in order to see Mrs. Muir because the doctor had told him she was not expected to live for more than a few months at the most. Kent, as he studied his sister's face, was not certain if she knew how serious her illness was, and how brief a time yet remained to her.

"Here is Brice," Mrs. Muir said softly as her only son entered the front room of their Florida bungalow. "You've not seen him, Kent, since he was ten or eleven years old, have you?"

Kent stepped back a few inches when he set eyes on his nephew, and his right hand moved slightly upwards as it did when he saluted an enlisted man.

"Here he is at last, your Uncle Kent." Mrs. Muir spoke to Brice as if her brother would not hear her prompting her son. Brice blushed a deep brick red, and looked away.

"Brice has so often spoken of you," Gladys Muir went on. "He has collected all the snapshots of you, and keeps them over his dresser. Especially the photo of you coming out from swimming in the ocean somewhere. That seems to be his favorite of you."

Brice turned his gaze to the patio outside, and colored even more violently. He was then just sixteen and was shy for his age.

"If Uncle Kent will excuse me, Mother, I have to practice my cornet. I have a lesson today," Brice apologized. He almost bowed to his uncle as he left the room.

Mrs. Muir and her brother laughed in agreeable nervousness as the boy took leave of them.

"Brice wears his hair quite long, doesn't he?" Ken remarked as they sat down, and began sipping some fresh lemonade.

Soon they could hear the cornet coming from the garage where Brice practiced.

"Say, he sounds like a real professional."

"He plays with a very fine group of musicians," Mrs. Muir said. "But after his father's death, you see, he left school. That was two or three years ago. He has been working in a restaurant days. He gets up every morning before five o'clock."

Her brother clicked his tongue.

Mrs. Muir observed then how very short Kent's own hair was, though he wore rather long and well-defined sideburns which emphasized his deep-set green eyes.

"He does so much want to be a musician, Kent." Mrs. Muir spoke as if giving away a secret.

"How much have you told Brice about everything, Gladys?" Kent wondered, wiping his mouth from the tart drink.

"Oh, nothing at all. He thinks I am just not feeling up to par."

"I understand," her brother said, looking at one of his fingernails which was blackened owing to his having caught it in his car door that day.

"Let me show you your room, Kent." Mrs. Muir led him up the brightly carpeted stairs. "You'll share the same bathroom with Brice, if you don't mind," she explained. "The bathroom which should be yours has been out of order for a few days. I hope this is agreeable."

When Brice came home from work in the restaurant in the late afternoon the next day, Kent was outside upon a ladder cleaning out the eaves of the roof. Owing to the sudden spell of hot weather, his uncle had taken off his shirt. He had worked so hard, repairing some of the broken parts of the eaves, and also fastening down some loose tiles on the roof, that rivulets of sweat poured down his chest to his bronzed thick arms.

"Need any help, Uncle Kent?" Brice called up to him, smiling broadly.

In answer, coming down from the ladder, Kent ruffled up the boy's thick mop of hair, and grinned.

"All fixed now, Brice, so the water won't run out the wrong way."

Brice avoided his uncle's glance, but smiled continually.

Mrs. Muir observed the two men from inside, where she sat on a new davenport she had purchased only a few days before. She smiled at seeing her brother and son together.

"Brice will be in good hands," Mrs. Muir spoke softly to herself. "Certainly strong ones."

Gladys Muir still did most of the housework, though the doctor had advised her against doing so. She always scrubbed the bathroom immaculately, for she felt Brice liked to see it sparkling clean. On the shelf above the washbasin, Mrs. Muir was accustomed to reach up and take down Brice's comb, in which every day four or five strands of his gold hair were left behind. She would remove the hair, and place it in a small box in her own bedroom.

But after Kent arrived, as she would go in to clean their common bathroom, she observed that there were no hairs now in the comb. The first time she noticed this, she stood for a long time staring at the comb. She lifted it up and looked under it. She felt then, strangely, unaccountably, as if a load had been lifted from her heart.

She found herself from then on waiting, one might say, for the ceremony of the cleaning of the bathroom and the looking at the comb. But with each passing day, every time she picked up the comb it was clean, without one hair remaining.

There was a small aperture leading from the bathroom to a closet down the hall, a kind of register which conveyed hot air from the furnace in winter. The next day, when she heard Kent go into the bathroom, she opened the air register. She was trembling so badly she was afraid he would hear her.

But Kent was completely occupied, she saw, in polishing his boots until they shone like a looking glass. But then, straightening up, she saw him gaze at Brice's comb. He took hold of it with extreme care. He was completely absorbed in looking at the comb which she could see still held a few of Brice's hairs in its teeth.

Kent held the comb for a while close to his mouth, then lowering it, almost languidly, he removed the strands of hair and placed them in his khaki shirt pocket.

Mrs. Muir stole away into her own bedroom, and sat down heavily. She could hear her brother in his own bedroom, moving about. He remained there for only a short time, then he went downstairs, got into his rented car, and drove away.

When she felt her strength return, Mrs. Muir went into Kent's bedroom. She made his bed, and did some dusting and sweeping. Then very slowly she advanced to the dresser and opened each drawer deliberately one after the other. She left the top drawer for last, as if she must prepare herself for what she would find in it. There was a small mother-of-pearl box there. She opened it. At first she saw only the reproduction on its underlid of a painting of John the Baptist as a youth. But in the box itself, arranged in pink tissue paper, she spied a gathering of the gold hair of Brice Muir. She closed the box. There was a kind of strange smile playing over all her features at that moment.

Mrs. Muir felt, she did not know why, the same way she had when her father, the day of her wedding, had held her arm and they had walked down the aisle of the church together, and her father had then presented her to her bridegroom. She had felt at the moment a kind of bliss. She now felt she could give up her son to someone who would cherish him as her bridegroom had cherished her.

But when Gladys Muir began to talk with Kent about her "going," her brother became taciturn and embarrassed, and the serious commitment she wished from him was not made.

The days passed, and Mrs. Muir realized that very little time remained. She knew positively that she had now only days, perhaps hours. The doctor had told her her passing would be so easy she would scarcely be aware of it, such was the nature of her malady.

As she felt then that the time for parting was imminent, she took Brice's comb in her handkerchief so that it could not be seen and joined Kent where he sat playing solitaire in the front room.

He stopped playing immediately she had come in, and stood up in a kind of military fashion. Brice was outside practicing his cornet in the garage, so of course he could not overhear what she might say, or what her brother might answer.

When Kent had put away his cards and was sitting on the new davenport facing her, Gladys Muir without warning brought out Brice's comb.

She saw the look of consternation on her brother's face.

"I want to tell you, Kent, how great a happiness I feel that you are close to my boy. The effort of speaking is very hard for me, as I believe I told you. So I have brought this to speak for me."

A deep silence prevailed.

"Take it, Kent, for I have an identical comb upstairs in my room."

Kent took the comb. His eyes filled with tears.

"You will keep him with you, Kent?" Gladys managed to say.

She was pleased, and grateful, to see how strong her brother's emotion was.

"I don't ever want to leave him," her brother got out. "But do you think he will want to be with me equally?"

"I know he will, Kent. He has a kind of worship of you, and always has. So you will have one another. . . . But what neither of you can know is the great burden that is being lifted from my heart knowing you will be close to one another."

"I will make him my life if he will let me." The uncle spoke in a kind of incoherent manner.

Mrs. Muir was sad she had forced it all upon him in so short a space, but then she saw that no other course would have been possible.

Kent was so blinded by his tears, tears really of joy, he later was to realize, and also tears of so many strange and powerful feelings, that it took him some time to look over at his sister and then to realize she had gone.

At the very moment of his realization he heard the cornet playing cease. He went to the door as Brice was coming through it. As if the boy read the meaning in his uncle's face, he put down his cornet, and threw himself into the older man's arms.

··*·*·*

There was almost no one at the funeral. There was the minister, and a woman who played the organ and who sang one song in a faded alto voice, and then of course the gravediggers and the sexton.

Brice had put on his best Sunday suit, a little too small for him, and a brand-new tie which his mother had purchased for him only last week. Uncle Kent wore his captain's uniform with several bright-colored citations across the jacket.

Kent noticed that Brice did not shed any tears at the service, and he looked very pale. His lips moved from time to time as if he was playing his cornet. They went to a very expensive restaurant later, but neither of them was able to eat very much. Neither Kent nor Brice drank at all, so there was nothing somehow to give them any kind of solace.

"I am going to take care of everything, Brice," Kent told him just before starting the motor of his car. "I don't want you to have to worry about the smallest detail."

It was only eight o'clock in the evening, but Brice said he must go to bed soon as he was due at the restaurant the next morning no later than five-thirty.

"You don't need to work there anymore, Brice," Kent said thickly as he sat on the new davenport. "Unless you want to, of course." He amended his statement when he saw a look of uneasiness on the face of his nephew. "I have enough, you see, for both of us."

"I think, Uncle Kent, it might get my mind off of everything if I did go to work just as usual."

"All right, Brice. But, remember, you don't have to. As I said, there's enough for both of us."

Kent stood up then, and made a motion to take Brice in his arms, but something in the way the young man looked at him caused him merely to shake hands with him and give him a husky good-night.

It began to rain outside, and presently there was a distant peal of thunder, and flashes of silver and sometimes yellow lightning. Kent closed the door leading to the patio. He took out a pack of worn cards, and began his game of solitaire.

All at once it seemed to him he could hear his sister's voice as she showed him the comb with the gold strands of hair.

"She knew everything and was glad," Kent said aloud. "But then, after all, I am his uncle, and too old for him."

⌁⌁⌁⌁⌁

The rain had wet the top blanket on his bed, so Kent threw this off. He had his small transistor radio and he decided he would just lie in bed and listen to some music.

The rain whipped against the roof and the windows. Kent felt very restless and edgy. His sister's sudden death did not seem real, and he kept seeing her showing him the comb. He could not believe Gladys had meant what she had said, but then what else could she have meant?

He had dozed off when a noise wakened him. It was, he soon realized, Brice taking a shower, and the sound of the water in the bathroom mingled with the sound of the steady downpour, outside, of the rain. He dozed off again, and then he thought he heard someone call. Rising up in bed, he saw that Brice had entered his room. He had no clothes on. At first the thought crossed the uncle's mind that he was walking in his sleep, but then he saw this was not true.

"Can I come in, Uncle Kent?" Brice's voice reached him as if it came from a far distance, and sounded like a small child's in the dark.

"Please, Brice."

"You don't ever drink or smoke, do you, Uncle Kent?"

The uncle shook his head. They both listened to the radio, which was playing a waltz.

"May I sit on the edge of your bed?" Brice inquired.

"You're crying," Kent said throatily. "And you're still wet from your shower."

"No, it's from the rain. I stepped out on the porch for a while. I felt so good with the rain coming down on me. . . . But I shouldn't get your bed wet."

"The rain got my top blanket wet also before I turned in," Kent explained.

He suddenly took Brice's outstretched hand in his.

"It's all right to cry in my presence," Kent said, but he had hardly got the words out before Brice threw himself into his uncle's arms. He began weeping convulsively, almost violently.

Kent held him to his chest tightly.

"You're shivering, Brice. Get under the covers for a while at least."

The boy obeyed, and Kent found himself holding him very tightly under the blanket as the boy sobbed on.

Kent all at once kissed the boy on his cheek, and as he kissed him some of the tears came into his mouth.

The sobs began to subside.

"I feel very close to you, Uncle Kent," Brice said. "Do you to me?"

"I do." Kent heard his own voice coming, it seemed, from beneath the floorboards, and unrecognizable as his own.

"I told my mother how I cared for you," Brice said, after a

considerable effort, and as he said this he kissed his uncle on the mouth and then let his lips rest there. "She told me to stay with you if you would want me to. She said you loved me."

"If I would want you to!" Kent spoke almost in high anguish, even deliriously.

"Yes, she thought you might."

"Oh, Brice," the uncle stammered, and he kept his mouth against the boy's. "If you care for me," Kent went on, "it will be beyond my wildest dream."

"Why is that, Uncle Kent?"

They kept their lips close together.

"Why is that?" the uncle repeated. He kissed him all over the face now.

"You are drying up all my tears," Brice told him.

Then: "I loved you when I first saw you, Uncle Kent," Brice whispered.

The uncle shook his head, but held the boy very close to him. He felt he was dreaming all this. No one had ever loved him before, neither women nor men. He had given up any hope of love. Then he had found his sister's boy's comb full of golden hair, and now he held this boy to his breast. It could not be true. He must be asleep, fast aslumber, or he was still across the ocean and his sister and her son whom he had so seldom seen were far away from him, unknown persons against time and distance.

Then he felt the boy's burning kisses on his body.

They grasped one another then with frantic passion, like men lost at sea who hold to one another before the final breaker will pass over them.

"Is this true, Brice?" Kent said after a while in the midst of such unparalleled joy. "Are you sure you want to be with me?"

Brice held his uncle in his desperate embrace, and kissed him almost brutally on the mouth.

"I said you had dried all my tears," Brice told him. He kissed his uncle again and again, and his hand pressed against the older man's thigh.

"I hope in the morning I will find you against my heart and it will not be just a thing I felt in slumber," Kent said.

He sensed his nephew's hot breath and wet kisses against his chest, and he plunged his thick stubby hard fingers through the mass of gold hair.

Outside, the lightning had turned to a peculiar pink, and the peals of thunder came then more threatening and if possible louder, and the rain fell in great white sheets against the house and the spattered windows.

THE FLOWERS OF
JEAN CHALEY
(1878–1960)

IMPORTANT PAINTINGS BY
FRENCH POST-IMPRESSION

, Maurer

y European Masters Thru Feb eger, Lissitzky, Grosz, Schwitters	
	To Feb 6
	To Jan 30
Prints relating to Broadway done f the Manhattan Graphics Center	
Exhibition (front gallery) To Jan 30	
k gallery)	

by Gallery Artists

re	Extended
	To Feb 3
	To Feb 9
n," Paintings	To Jan 30
ture	To Jan 30
	To Jan 30

About the Author

James Purdy was born and raised in the Midwest. His first book of fiction, 63: Dream Palace, was published in England in 1957. Since then, Purdy has written numerous novels, plays, poetry, and short stories, including Malcolm, Eustace Chisholm and the Works, In a Shallow Grave, The House of the Solitary Maggot, On Glory's Course, and, most recently, In the Hollow of His Hand. James Purdy lives in New York City.